"Read  memories of when I lived on the old Lorett Homestead from 1931 to 1948. We drank the same spring water as our ancients found in the Cherokee Outlet land run of '93. Brushie Holler was my favorite to hide away the hours from all the work, work, work required of that ole sandhill farm. Of course we didn't have any gas, electricity, running water; we cut wood for heat and to feed that cook stove. We were never alone; our animals provided us with company as did our neighbors. I'm sure the hardships we had could not compare to those that have gone on before us. These memories brought back the tears and a lot of laughs."

Cousin Jack Lorett

Thanks to my brother Pat for the stirring account of early day struggles between pioneers and Native Americans. He has done a marvelous job and provided rich insights into the long-forgotten attitudes of early day settlers toward the Indians and mixed races of Oklahoma Territory. I don't remember my Grandma Josie ever sitting with empty hands. She always had sewing in them, including knitting, mending, tatting, and crocheting. Her prized Singer (sewing machine) was often working a mile a minute. Wonder how many miles she put on it? Through it all she kept her family clean and well-fed and still had time to help a neighbor in need. She always made time to help with birthing babies, even when she had to give an expecting mom a bath before she helped deliver a new baby. I'll always remember her beautiful soft skin. She made us all toe the line and wear a hat or bonnet. Never let the sun touch your skin, she said, and, 'Don't let the sun blister.' I can hear her still. Don't slump, stand tall, and hold your head high, she would say. Read your Bible ever day for the teaching of Jesus.' I still have her old Bible. I can't read the tiny print anymore, but I remember her motto in life, John 6:35. It says, Jesus said unto them, I am the bread of life; he who comes to Me shall not hunger, and he who believes in Me shall never thirst. She believed it and I believe it too.

Sister Ruth Lorett Moffatt

"*To My Own Home* is a collection of stories about my tough-as-nails, Sooner great-grandmother, Josephine Lorett. Grandma Josie died the year before I was born, so I'm delighted to finally meet her through the writings of her eighteenth grandchild, Pat Lorett. His stories paint a vivid picture of her life of hard work and faith in God. So sit a spell, read along, you'll be glad to have met her and those who wrested their living from those acres near the Cimarron River. Josie would have been pleased to know that her legacy of faith has been embraced by her 'grands' and is now being shared with other folks as well."

Niece Linda (Lorett) McIntyre

TO MY OWN
HOME

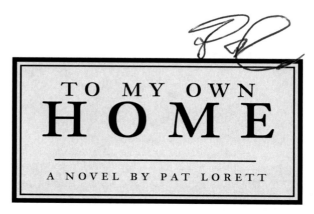

TO MY OWN
HOME

A NOVEL BY PAT LORETT

Oct. 20, 2008

To Ray & Jean, we hope
you enjoy reading this
one, too.

Pat & Shorty

TATE PUBLISHING & *Enterprises*

Published by Tate Publishing & Enterprises, LLC
127 E. Trade Center Terrace | Mustang, Oklahoma 73064 USA
1.888.361.9473 | www.tatepublishing.com

Tate Publishing is committed to excellence in the publishing industry. The company reflects the philosophy established by the founders, based on Psalm 68:11,
"The Lord gave the word and great was the company of those who published it."

Published in the United States of America

ISBN: 978-1-60604-939-6
1. Fiction: Historical/Oklahoma
2. Biography & Autobiography
08.08.20

TABLE OF CONTENTS

TRIALS

"Breed! Breed! Breed!" That was all I could remember. I had been put out of the circle so much that life's hardship was the way I existed. Both races shunned me as if I were diseased; I had grown to young womanhood with my white mother until she couldn't handle the talk. The tribe wasn't any better with their names. I had tried to give up, but my spirit forced me into countless fights. This time was different; I scratched, clawed, hissed, and was knocked about by the braves so much that my face became a mess of bruises. I woke up to an old Indian woman wiping the blood away. I withdrew to my drawn-up sitting position. They could beat me all they wanted to now that I've got my face hid. A simple croon sound kept ringing inside the teepee. I realized my eyes were swollen shut and I couldn't see. I was given water and dried meat. The meat and drink sated my emptiness, the stupor was a welcomed sleep, then that hide blanket put over my body kept me as still as a mouse.

Sounds of waking in the camp stirred my keeper to build a fire. As she prepared some food, I realized I was empty again. She came and uncovered me and motioned for me come eat my fill. I didn't have a clue what she said, but I stuffed so much in my mouth, I almost gagged. I was famished, cold, tired, dirty, and sleepy; as I fell over on my hide blanket, she covered up my head, neck, and ears, and I was dead asleep again.

The ritual played out over two days; I became aware of the strange smell of drying plants. I got one of my eyes open enough to see my keeper and realized I was in the teepee of the healer. I could smell roast meat; the offer was put in my hand, and I wolfed down a whole rabbit carcass, picked the bones, and drank my fill. I felt cleaner and found I had been washed and dressed in an Indian dress all the way to my feet. I tried to smile and cracked a lip; a coating from an undistinguishable plant soothed the pain. My keeper never changed her style; she always tended to my needs, crooning all the while. I tried to stand, which didn't work, as I swooned back on my hide blanket. A faint smile looked down on me, and gentle hands gave me some drink out of a wooden bowl. The teepee spun around once and I was out of sight again.

The teepee kept turning and left me lying on my sweat-soaked blanket, my head seemed clearer as my keeper floated around, continuing to croon. I felt like I had been asleep one whole moon by the time I was fully awake. This time the offering was some watery soup that I devoured in one gulp, with more water, and I asked the keeper her name. I got no answer, as if she did not hear me. I smiled a little, and a jolt of pain reminded me not to. She smiled back, and I knew immediately I was in the right place to receive help. My keeper imitated walking with her fingers and brought an imaginary drink to her lips—her way of suggesting we should go for a walk to get some water, let's go for a walk and get some water. My bones hurt, my muscles were weak, I hurt all over, and she wanted to walk?

Again she signed to walk.

I asked her name and she signed, "Raven." I tried but couldn't remember what the sign for my name was, and then Raven signed, "Use this shoulder wrap." She put her fingers to her lips, warning me not to say a word, and she stepped out in the cold morning air.

Raven led the way to a large spring and stopped to pull sage and dig garlic. I helped when I could, but the ground was a long way down. We filled her hide bag with water and were treading the way back to her teepee when a gang of ruffian braves stopped us. They didn't have the courage to dismount; they just circled, screaming their war cry. I melted down on the ground and covered up my head. Not a word was spoken by Raven, but her signing hand made its wave and a dip. Almost immediately the attack dissolved in the trailing dust. I peered out just in time to see their backsides and hear them trying to laugh the charge off. I wondered right then, *Who am I staying with? They are afraid of Raven!*

We made it back to the teepee, and lying right in front of the flap was a freshly killed rabbit. I was so tired from the excursion that I flopped down on my hide blanket and was instantly asleep.

Dreams, ghosts, dragons, bats, all hurling fire darts at me, woke me, drenched in sweat, with my keeper wiping my sore face with a cool animal skin. I could smell the roasting rabbit and saw a hide bag full of watery soup with cooking stones. I got more water down.

"Let's have something to eat," Raven signed.

I ate my fill. I heard some noise outside, and Raven lifted the flap of the teepee to find an old Indian man with a cut on his leg. Raven turned healer and had him sit on the hearthstone while she cleaned his leg with the same plant she put on my lip. She gave him some of that sweet-smelling cup I had gotten, and he went limp in her arms. Long horsehair stitched the flesh back together without a whimper from his lips. I became aware of the rasping sounds coming from the old Indian's breathing. Raven listened to his chest and rolled him over; the rasping stopped, and color returned to his face.

Raven signed, "I have to see about something. If the rasping returns, move him around till it quits."

I stayed on my watch, and, sure enough, that old rasping sound gave its noise. I did just like Raven signed, which provided instant relief. The old brave began coming around and was aware that I was giving him some water. I noticed he was covered with scars of wars past. He tried to talk with me, but his language was foreign.

"Who are you?" he signed.

I knew my white man's names could not be signed. Finally, I hummed him a song and he returned to his nap. Raven lifted the flap, and I realized she had been there all the time. Raven looked at me, satisfied that now was the time to fill me in.

"Thank you, Josie. You will make a good midwife." She spoke perfect English!! I looked at her with the sternest look I could muster and demanded to know why she had only signed to me.

"Josie, where you are going, you will need to know both languages. I had to see what you could do before going any farther."

My education continued that day, with Raven as my teacher.

Hard Knock School

I had been put out of the white man's race because of my skin color—brown—yet I had eye color that kept me out of the Indian race—blue. Raven, my teacher, took on a ragamuffin young woman rejected by both races and could see a glimmer of hope for a midwife. I was shy, backward, scared of the dark and anything that moved, with the most helpless of attitudes. Not to be put off, my teacher nursed me back to health with nothing but food and understanding. As the days warmed, we spent more time hunting for spices, herbs, and roots, and Raven taught me the names of each plant.

As long as I was with my mentor, the attacks grew less and less and finally stopped altogether. One day I asked why the braves wanted to harm me. Raven smiled so sweetly, then she told me about the culture barrier I was to face.

"Those young braves are scared of anything that

is different, Josie. Remember where they always hit you?"

"Y-y-yes," I stammered. "They pounded my face!"

"Yes, that's where you are different from any Indian woman. You're so fine-featured. Those blue eyes are the color of the sea and limitless in depth. Those braves were scared to be around you."

"Raven, what were the signs you gave to that rowdy bunch?"

She chuckled and told me the superstitions of ancient past.

"The story hides of long ago tell of medicine men who could predict the future, when it would happen, and to whom. The people at that time worshiped the sun. They had all kinds of satanic rituals, even cut themselves to please the gods. All they accomplished was a dying off of the leaders of the tribes, leaving the tribes without any leadership or direction. It was left open to strange leaders. Josie, remember this day forever. I will be gone in time. Learn all you can from each experience, and in time you will use that information."

I learned the silent sign language from Raven, how to name all the herbs, when to heal the sick, when and where to be silent or speak up, and when to leave.

Raven didn't wake the next morning. I shook her cold body and wept drops of leaving tears. I dressed in my old dress and put my buckskins over them, taking what I would need to survive for several days. I stepped out in the predawn never to be in the Indian way of life again. I traveled upstream from camp and hid in some cliffs along a large river. I saw several groups of braves and figured they were hunting for me. A large fire in the predawn the next morning told me the camp of Indians was stricken. I waited for the next dawn and made my way back to the camp. Sure enough, Raven's teepee had been burnt to the ground. I knew the tribe would never come this way again, and I sifted through the remains for Raven. The only thing I could find were her scull and teeth; I pondered this action and buried them in the sand along the river. I felt the tribe would never want to know about Raven or what she meant to me.

CHANGING RACES

I slipped back into the white man's realm by traveling east and following the rivers. I wore the buckskins until I was ready to meet the crowds, washing the dress while taking a bath in the river. I asked at a trading post and found out I was close to my mother's town of Braymer, Missouri. A bonnet hid my black hair and high cheekbones, while listening filled me in on the news.

I found Mother's house, but the people coming and going told me that my mother had moved away. I found the old church where I was confirmed, and, lo and behold, my old priest was still on duty. I asked for a confessional and gained the audience of the Father. I confessed to the priest of my sins of the past, and the kindly priest called me by name and told of missing me in church. I didn't tell him I had been living with the Indians, but I felt he knew. He asked what I intended to do, and I told him I was trying to fit back into the white man's race. He had me come and stay with the nuns, for he was sure something would come up I could do. I worked in the gardens and stable of the convent, doing a lot of things that most people wouldn't have done, but I enjoyed the animals and the outside air. I fell into a pattern of helping do whatever needed to be done, and I worked for my food.

I felt I was at a crossroad as I attended the next mass. A kindly gentleman named Mr. Olaf Bigla asked the priest if he knew of anyone who could take care of his wife, Bessie. The priest said he knew of a young woman, and a deal was struck that day for me to have a place in the white man's realm. From that day forward, I knew the training Raven had given me would be needed for the rest of my life. I moved my meager belongings to a plantation on the outskirts of town. Miss Bessie, as they called her, was paralyzed on one side of her body and would never speak or walk again.

I tended the woman and got back into the rhythm of life as her nurse. We had a terrible time talking, but I felt her mind was still intact but was locked up in silence. I began signing, and she soon got caught up with Indian sign language. We got to where we could sign to each other, and her mind took on an all-new understanding. I found a very educated lady with an immense knowledge of life. From that time forward she practiced constantly with her paralyzed hand; the whole of her left side was pulled out of shape. She never asked why I had all the facial scars, as we met on common ground.

I had plenty of spare time and filled the days with mending clothes about the kitchen and house. Miss Bessie seemed upset to see me doing such a menial job, and I finally caught on that there was a machine that would help me out. Mr. Bigla came, and Miss Bessie tried to tell him what she wanted. I tried to translate to no avail. I got every book, magazine, and pamphlet until I found a book on sewing machines. The biggest smile came on my patient as she signed for her husband to go to Braymer and order one. I saw the price and blanched at the thought of spending thirty-one dollars for a machine when I could sew by hand. The machine was ordered, and I forgot about the incident. I busied myself with the days, and a fine young man came one day with a new Singer Treadle machine. It was set up beside the bed of Miss Bessie and the salesman demonstrated the stitches it would make. I made up my mind that day never to use anything that took my eyes, hands, and feet to make a stitch.

Miss Bessie, not to be put off, kept the idea in front of me until I felt I could at least unfold the top. I found an intimidating, shiny black iron machine. She got the picture out, and I learned to set up the machine and string the belt. Threading took a while longer, and I was satisfied to dust the monster. I did mend a pot holder one day by turning the wheel on top. I took my project to the kitchen and looked over the stitch while out of everyone's sights. I took my worst fears back to that infernal hunk of iron and, in Cherokee, told it I was going to master its internal workings! This seemed to soothe the savage beast in me, and I started right in trying to sew a straight seam. I got to the edge of the material and ran out of thread! I happened to look at Miss Bessie, and she was having the laugh of the day—not at me, but at the hunk of iron. With Miss Bessie's help I was able to tread Blackie, as I called it, and start mending in earnest. As Blackie and I agreed that we would laugh at the first attempts and then make do from then on. I gave up on hand mending, and we agreed to work together.

Never did Bessie ask me about my dark face or black hair. Her husband of fifty years was delighted at the progress we were making. I always attended early mass, and it became so easy to get me back into the everyday run of life. With my head covered with a white veil, I grew confident that I could make the white man's life my own. The kindly Mr. Olaf Bigla started me writing again; my first attempts were such a mess, but I kept at it till I got my thoughts down. My keeper gave me a leather-bound journal for bookkeeping. Those red lines kept my pencil between them.

"Oh, one more thing, Miss Josephine Smith. You call me Olaf from now on, and I will call you Josie."

"Oh, Olaf, that sounds so common, but I'll do as you say."

My charge was chipper this morning after I attended mass. She wanted to know who was there and who wasn't. I didn't have a clue who "they" were, but I answered some of the names that I remembered: Lorett, Clawson, Jasper, and several others.

"Oh, yes," she signed, "I remember that family of Loretts. They have several children about your age."

I made a mental note to check them out from the back row next mass.

Bessie's afternoon nap was restless, with snoring that made the windows rattle. I thought through my training with Raven and remembered the plant that would soothe the mind. I asked my master if I could go walking out in the forest and waterways. He gladly gave me free run of his country estate. As I slipped out in to the afternoon sun, my Indian training took over in a heartbeat. I heard all the raucous calls of the forest, found a good creek to cool my feet in, and just let my spirits mingle with the earth's feelings. I found all my old herbs and named them in my mind's refreshed state. I didn't find the soothing herb until I heard the farm hogs grunting their welcome. I remember then that the mind-soothing herb only grew around the droppings of hogs. I wondered if I should give my charge a small portion of the herb called Sang. Oh well, she can't talk or walk and surely I can handle the situation

I requested a small building from Olaf to dry my herbs. The groundskeeper made me some drying racks, and I was back in the business of medicinal herbs. For the life of me I couldn't think of the mind-soothing herb, but Sang seemed all right. My charge got her portion for lunch that day. I watched her ever so closely during naptime. All the pulled wrinkles smoothed, and she slept the sleep of exhaustion. I made the mental note to be very careful. After her nap, the wrinkles stayed away for a few hours, and she even made some crooning sounds to me. Reminded me of the hours that Raven had crooned to help me sleep.

Olaf came up to the bedroom and beamed with delight at the progress his wife was making. I asked to open the bedroom and air out the dampness that had accumulated.

"No, no, Josie. The doctor said to keep the sunlight out of her eyes."

I kept his wish and wondered if the doctor could be wrong. I opened the windows and cooled the room some. By dark those old wrinkles and that pulled face came back to my patient, and she became silent. Olaf told me to take the next day off, and he would do the nursing. I changed into my outside clothes and dust apron and made for the cool forest.

August in Missouri is always still, humid, and hot. I soon shed my apron, made it into a carrying basket, and filled it to the flap with plants to dry. I detoured by the pigpen to restock with Sang. The pigs met me squealing like only pigs can expecting their daily ration, and I noticed they were out of water and feed. I hand-pumped water to sate their thirst, but I could not find any feed. The only thing I could see was some standing ear corn, and I threw stalks and all into their pen. I left them to their *grunt chomp chomp* and thought to myself, *Those pigs need more feed.* I arrived back at the mansion just as the groundskeeper told Olaf that somebody had been throwing cornstalks into the pigpen. I quickly took my full dust apron in my drying house and listened to what was going on. I peeked through the cracks in the door, and, lo and behold, the groundskeeper was *drunk!* I thought on this and heard Olaf tell him not to worry, for he would find out who was wasting the corn. The air cleared somewhat, and I ventured back to the house and got caught coming in the back door by Olaf himself. I thought my employment would be finalized soon.

"Miss Josie, we need to talk," came from the master as I quaffed a large drink of water.

"Olaf, it was I who fed those pigs; they were out of feed and water, and I felt sorry for them."

"Wait, wait, Miss Josie, I know all about those pigs. You were the only one out in the forest, and I thank you for feeding my porkers. I have been hearing them squeal for food for some time and haven't been able to get out there and see what is going on. My grounds-keeper has been coming to work slightly inebriated; as the day went on it gets worse. I noticed that the pigs got quiet, and I dismissed the thought until you were out in the forest and he came and told about somebody throwing cornstalks in their pen. I put two and three together, and my groundskeeper must have another business on the side. Now, Miss Josie, go on about your usual chores with my Bessie, and I will come up with a plan to find out what is going on in my forest."

Whew! That was close. I thought I had lost my job over a mess of hogs. Miss Bessie was restless this morning, and I tried everything I could think of to soothe her mind until I fixed her dinner. I wondered if I should try the Sang again. I had given her an ever-so-small pinch in her tea, and it lasted for several hours. I decided I would never know unless I tried. Miss Bessie didn't want much except her tea and toast and quickly fell into a deep slumber. Olaf asked about Bessie, and I said she was resting quietly.

"You know, Miss Josie, we need to talk some more about my problem out in the forest. Let's go make us some mint tea, go out on the veranda, and we'll talk."

I could see that I was going to be questioned and was determined to tell the truth.

The talk session started with the telling about Olaf's groundskeeper.

"He has been on the estate for many years and all in all is worth his keep. Recently his work has been out in the forest, and the grounds have taken on a shoddy look. Then his nose told the story that he was taking on more drink than could be bought by his salary. I hate to fire a good helper, but he has become a bit of a problem."

As my keeper went on, he sighed ever so slightly and then began again.

"Miss Josie, there is more to you than you are letting on. You are very good help with my Bessie; in fact, you are better at nursing her, well, than the doctor I have hired. Take today for instance. Bessie was very restless last night, and now you have her asleep by just making those crooning sounds. Miss Josie, you tell me about your life and it will not go past my lips."

It was my turn to sigh, and the telling was very hard.

"Olaf, yes, there is more to me than you know, but the telling will not help your wife one jot or tittle. Your wife is mute from now on and will never get past the crooning sound that you have heard. I only help her to relax the muscles that pull on the side of her face, and then she can make a singing sound. I have taught her the sign language of the Indians, and we talk like two crows on a fence."

"Yes," he mused, "that is a miracle. Where did you learn sign language?"

I gulped at being caught, and Olaf said quietly, "Miss Josie, don't say a word. You don't have to tell me anything you don't want to. I can see that you are an Indian or at least part; you have the most beautiful blue eyes. You speak with such eloquence that I know that you have been around someone who spoke proper English. All this don't bother me one speck. I just want to know, how do you help my Bessie?"

Some singsong that Miss Bessie was humming interrupted us. As we made our way back into the bedroom, she was beaming from refreshed sleep, signing to bring some of that mint tea, and to talk where she could hear what was being said.

I almost had to tell the whole story but was rescued by Miss Bessie! Olaf held his wife so tenderly and told her all that was happening on the estate. I noticed that the groundskeeper fiasco never came up.

Olaf came the next morning and wanted breakfast with his wife. I fixed them tea with some sweet bread. The old pulled muscles were back, and Miss Bessie was beginning to be in pain again. I tried to soothe her, but it was not to be. Olaf said he would go to town to get the doctor. Olaf seemed to be in pain at the decision he had to make. I kept quiet and never asked if I could help. The groundskeeper never came around that morning, and I had put the problem aside until I heard the ruckus start out by the barn. Olaf Bigla had been out in the forest and had caught the keeper making whiskey and feeding the leftover mash to his hogs. The hogs loved the swell and were not feeling any pain when the evil deed was discovered. I thought Olaf was in trouble until I saw his 30–30 saddle gun in ready position. I trembled at the thought and hid myself in the bedroom with Miss Bessie. She was in a signing mood and wanted to talk the hours away. I dreaded going to see what was happening when I heard the groundskeeper wagon going down the lane toward town. Olaf came, greeted his wife with a kiss, and said he wanted to talk with me after dinner and instructed me not to go out in the forest for a while. Miss Bessie made the most of dinner, and I never gave her any Sang that day.

I woke in the night with Miss Bessie trying her singsong song, but all that came out was the gurgle from pulled muscles. I relented and made her the tea and toast that she liked, and I relied on a slight pinch of herb. It wasn't thirty minutes before she settled into her relaxed state and slept the most perfect sleep. I dozed in the side chair and woke to Olaf standing beside his mate, watching her sleep; his smile was worth all the effort. He signaled for breakfast. As I thought about the night, I hoped that the doctor didn't find Miss Bessie relaxed.

Olaf started right in with the problems of his groundskeeper and how hard it was to run him off. I sympathized with him and volunteered to feed the hogs if he could find some feed.

"Now, Miss Josie, you are hired to take care of my Bessie. I can't have you going out in the forest taking care of a bunch of hogs."

"I fed hogs when I was growing up with my mother, and I kind of enjoy the ole porkers."

"Well, okay, but you be real careful for a while, because the groundskeeper had starved them to get them to eat the mash from the still."

"That's not a problem, Olaf. I can take care of myself. I wished later that I had not told him that. I checked in on Miss Bessie, and I instructed him to give her some tea if she awoke. The trip to the hog pen was just a few minute's walk, and I could hear them making their grunting sounds. My Indian senses took over, and I realized I was not alone in the forest. Mr. Groundskeeper was packing his still! I stepped one step too far and was discovered by the half-drunken sot.

"Well, lookie har," he slurred. "If it ain't the kitchen help to make me some breakfast. Come right into my camp and get busy, Miss Upitty-up."

I felt I was in no danger and went right to work fixing something to eat for the dirty ole man. His coffee can was just that, a can to boil water. I didn't say a word; I just made like I was at my everyday work. What he didn't know was I had fixed more meals over a campfire than ever in a kitchen. He got his greasy plate and spoon ready for his bacon and eggs. I made the coffee, and while he was busy, I slipped a double portion of Sang in his cup! He ate like the pigs: *slurp, grunt, squeal,* and then demanded more. I tended the fire as he started his midmorning nap that would last all day. Sure as anything, I had the whole forest to myself to make my getaway. I fed the hogs a double portion of slop and threaded my way back to the mansion, making sure that ole Mr. Groundskeeper was snoring.

As I made my way in the back door, the doctor was coming down the stairway. I could hear laughter upstairs and could just imagine the way Miss Bessie was acting. I looked at the doctor, the doctor looked at me, and we were both surprised.

"You're an Indian!" we said in unison. The doctor very quietly said, "We need to talk!"

I hung my head and could only look embarrassed. Olaf came in; he was bubbly about how good his wife felt this morning.

"Miss Bessie's face is as pretty as old times, and she can speak some."

I hated to give Mr. Olaf Bigla the news; there was an issue out in the forest that needed his attention. I told him about the drunken groundskeeper, how he had made me fix his breakfast, and that he was passed out on the ground. Olaf could sure change his gaiety to a more serious tone. The doctor suggested that the groundskeeper was trespassing on private land and that the constable should be notified.

"Yes, that is the best approach to a delicate problem. You two visit, and I'll get the authorities."

The doctor didn't seem to be in any hurry to leave, and I offered to prepare him some breakfast, to which he amiably agreed. We exchanged some Indian glances, signed to each other, and I settled down to the doctor talking.

"Miss Josie, I can only guess what's going on here in the Bigla house. I want to tell you a story. You just listen.

"When I was eight or nine years old, the old Indians ruled the tribes in the south. We had a very comfortable lifestyle. We even had slaves, of that I was not proud, but that was the way life was. I was educated in the best of schools and sent away to study medicine. This kept me out of the Indian wars and conflict with the white man. After my internship, I couldn't find any of my family. I think they were forced into the Indian Territories. Josie, where did you come from?"

I sat down at the same table and buried my scarred face in my hands.

"Oh, Josie, you don't have to tell me anything you don't want to. Just you think about it for a while."

I thought about my life and how messed up it was and wanted to melt in my seat.

"Josie, it's not your fault those bucks beat your face. You were just trying to stay alive!"

How did he know about the bucks? Where had he been all my life? Who did he think he was?

As the sobs subsided, I was able to collect myself enough to tell the doctor where I had been. I guess I needed to tell my story to someone, and the doctor had willing ears. The story included why I was part Indian and having to live with both races. I told him about the woman who had nursed me back to life and, upon her death, having to run away and hide. I had found my way back to my hometown in Missouri, and through the priest, Mr. Bigla had given me the job of nursing Miss Bessie.

All this seemed to jog the doctor's memory, and he told me a story that had run in his tribe about a healer named Raven. She was known to know all the herbs in the field, could heal all kinds of sickness, and was a revered leader among her tribe. The only trouble, the last anyone knew, was that she was getting old. I was holding my head in my hands all the time the doctor was talking about Raven. I know that my complexion was blanched; I couldn't have said a word without giving myself away when Mr. Bigla came running in the back door wanting to see the doctor. Seemed the constable had come and picked up the groundskeeper but couldn't wake him from his stupor. The doctor went outside to see his new patient and pronounced his bulk in a whiskey-induced sleep. I hurriedly went to see about Miss Bessie and found her asleep. I regained my normal color and came back to the kitchen as Mr. Bigla and the doctor returned. They were talking about the current turn of events and what needed to be done to resolve the hardship. They forgot about me as I returned to the nursing needs of my Miss Bessie.

I took over the feeding of the hogs, and they became my best listening friends in the forest. I would talk to them and practice all my different languages, including signing. One of them had a sore foot, and Olaf helped me remove a thorn. I guessed the seed was planted about me being able to help man or beast.

The grounds began to look unkempt, so we received a new groundskeeper in the form of a fine young man who spoke English and German. I lost my job feeding the pigs but was still free to visit them. Miss Bessie and I still talked by signing, and we had plenty to talk about. Olaf would speak aloud to her, and she would beam with plenty of expression. She grew less and less dependant on Sang as I weaned her down to strong tea. Her face smoothed out as practice talking used those drawn-up muscles. The groundskeeper seemed to appreciate his meals in the kitchen, and Olaf and Alex spoke their business of the plantation during meals. They seemed to like old-fashioned food, so I supplied their every need.

The doctor came one day, talked to Olaf, and he readily agreed as they came into the kitchen, the doctor wanted to talk to me in his office. I looked somewhat sheepishly. Olaf told me I didn't have to go if I didn't want to. I finally agreed to go if Olaf would let Alex look after Miss Bessie. We chatted on the way to the office about a man with a stroke. The doctor wanted me to examine his jaw and see if I knew what could be done. The man turned out to be the town mayor, and sure enough he was paralyzed on the right side of his face. I went in with the doctor, and he introduced me as "Nurse." The man was scared to death of having two Indians in the office with him. He soon got over his fears as I massaged his jaw.

"Mayor, try to relax, and the paralysis will go away in time. This sometimes happens. Not to worry."

We could see the man relax and left much relieved.

"Josie, let's have a cup of coffee. I want you to tell me about your time with Raven."

I covered up my face with my hands, and the doctor told me again that I didn't have to tell him anything I didn't want to. I settled down, uncovered my face, and told him all I knew about the woman Raven and my learning time with her. The doctor explained that he knew about the old healer and that he wanted to know what I had given Miss Bessie to help her paralysis. He also wanted to know what I had given the groundskeeper to put him asleep. I pondered for a while and told him I didn't want to tell.

"Okay, Miss Josie, I respect you for what you have done. Now what is wrong with my other patient?"

"Doctor, when a man gets fat, they sometimes gets palsy in the face muscles, and all you have to do is get the man to relax and the palsy will slowly go away."

"Okay, Miss Josie, that will help me. Now I want to help you. Miss Josie, do you want some help with those white scars on your face?"

I covered my face again and wept unashamed at the way I looked. The doctor sat in front of me and told me to let him see the scars, and then he told me something I would remember the rest of my life.

"Miss Josie, those scars, and the fact you are part Indian, are not your fault. You didn't have any choice in your parents; they were responsible for the mixture of blood. Now those scars are the result of those young men who were scared of your good looks. Miss Josie, I want to make a deal with you. If you will tell me what you gave Miss Bessie and that drunken sot to calm them down, I will try to repair the damage to your face so nobody will know the difference."

The very thought of repairing my face made me cry again, and I just couldn't think straight. I asked the doctor to take me back to the mansion and my work. I would think on the proposal. We arrived at the mansion in time to fix supper; I made fry bread and beans to the delight of all the men folk. They ate until they couldn't, while I took Miss Bessie supper and settled her in for the night.

I went to early mass the next daylight and received a request of the priest to speak with him.

"Miss Josie, my cow is having a time birthing. Can

you help her? Mr. Bigla told me that you were good with man or beast."

I immediately went to the barn of the poor beast; she had been in labor most of the night and was so weak. I found the calf breached and moved it forward enough to get a hold of its nose. We soon had a nice heifer calf much to the relief of the cow and the priest. The priest poured water on my hands to wash them. The cow was soon on its feet, and the calf was doing a good job slurping. I said that I must get back to Miss Bessie and fix breakfast. The priest made me promise to talk to him soon. I wondered why all those people wanted to talk with an Indian woman? All I did was help with a birthing. What was the big deal?

I came in just in time to make breakfast for the menfolk, and Olaf asked me how the cow was doing. I hung my head to hide my scars and remembered what the doctor had told me; it was not my fault my face was scarred. I looked Olaf in the face and told him the cow was fine and the heifer calf was nursing when I left. Then it struck me; he already knew about the priest's cow being in trouble and that I would help.

"Miss Josie, I want to talk to you when I get back from town. I think I need to know something."

What have I done now? Nothing! I will hold my head up high! I thought.

My morning rounds with Miss Bessie found her much improved. She wanted to sit in the morning sun for a while. I got Alex to help, and we fixed her a place so she could see all the backyards. She chatted with her hands while I changed all the linen. As Mr. Bigla drove in with his surrey, she waved her best.

Fatigue soon took its turn with Miss Bessie, and we

put her down for a morning nap. I fixed Mr. Bigla a tea, and he insisted that I join him in the breakfast nook.

"Olaf, I want to talk to you. I'm having trouble calling you Olaf. I want to call you Mr. Bigla."

He relented as I tried to act bashful, but I remembered the doctor's statement (*"Not your fault, Josie."*). I looked the gent in the face and reminded him he wanted to talk with me.

"Miss Josie, I want to tell you something that has been on my mind, and after talking with the doctor, I want you to let the doctor help you with your scars."

I almost covered my face but caught myself. "Mr. Bigla, I don't have the money to have that done."

"Yes, I understand that, but I want to pay the doctor. All you need to do is go to the doctor's office and take the treatments."

I couldn't help myself; I cried and sobbed till quiet.

"Mr. Bigla, you don't have to help me. I can take care of myself!"

"Yes, you can take care of yourself, I know that, but I want to help you."

"Mr. Bigla, I will pay you back."

"No, I want to do this for you, just because it's you."

I had never had anybody want to help me just because. I knew at that moment I would give in to the doctor's request. Mr. Bigla told me that he was hiring more kitchen help and was sending me a new girl to help with Miss Bessie. He was going to have a butcher come out from town to take care of the hogs.

"Whew! That will help!" I muttered to myself.

Early mass came and went without a word from the priest. I did notice a bouncing heifer calf in his stock pen. I was leaving when the priest caught me and thanked me for the donation to the orphans. I almost looked down and then looked the priest in the face and saw thanks in his eyes. *Mr. Bigla did it again!* I tried to explain, and the priest caught me in mid-sentence.

"Child, blessings come in the most unexplainable ways. Just take them and praise the Lord!"

I could see that the priest knew the whole story.

Change of Face

The doctor took me in the late evenings for my treat-ments. He covered my face with a towel and started right in with the first skin treatment. I wondered what could be done in such a short time. My bandage covered my whole face, and he told me not to peek; he would change them after two days. I went home thinking that nothing had been done, but the stinging started some-time before daylight. I almost took the bandages off and treated myself, but I didn't. I fixed meals, and my new kitchen help, Sue, served Miss Bessie; of course, she wanted to see me, and I finally went to her. She held me so tenderly I could have cried aloud. She made the most beautiful crooning noises; I wondered who was blessed.

The treatments went on for a whole month. My face turned as white as any white woman you'd ever see. The doctor helped me both physically and mentally by telling me the scars were disappearing ever so slowly. I didn't know how much he charged Mr. Bigla, but a deal was struck and I was going through with it

The mayor slowly regained the use of his face, and he came to the doctor's office one evening to talk to me. My first reaction was to hide from his eyes, but the doctor helped me and said the mayor knew all that he knew. We shared the feelings that we were going to need help the rest of our lives. He thanked me for massaging his jaw, and I thanked him for not saying anything bad about my face.

"Miss Josie, as mayor, you saw me at my worst and never let on that it made a speck of difference. I saw you as very talented healer who needed some help, and now it is your turn to accept my thanks."

The doctor finished with my treatments and said the rest was up to me. I should not let the sun get too hot on my face, and it would eventually turn back to its normal color. I got to looking in the mirrors in the mansion and noticed that, yes, my complexion was much better. Then I realized that I had never looked in those big mirrors! All the menfolk in my life had never paid much attention, much to my relief, as I gained self-esteem. I even got on with planning my life and dreamed of living in this mansion the rest of my normal years, which was not to be.

As winter took its grip on the weather, Mr. Bigla hired another helper to help keep the house warm. All the fireplaces had to be tended constantly to keep the chill off. I kept Sue busy with the housework. We cooked all the meals on a wood cookstove, and I healed up the best I could. I had been treating my face with oil from a plant that grew along the streams. I dried more herbs, made enough Sang to last a whole year, and got acquainted with Alex Lorett. All our meals were eaten

in the breakfast nook. Mr. Bigla dropped in occasion-
ally; he, and Alex always talked with fervor about the
plantation. I took on more responsibility with Miss
Bessie, and she started to walk some with a stand that
Alex had built. It was like a tall chair with sides on it
that Miss Bessie could slide along the floors. Mr. Bigla
was so proud of the progress his wife was having with
nothing but nursing as a guide.

TRUTH IS KNOWN

Mr. Bigla came with a lawyer one day and wanted Alex and me to meet with them in the study. He wanted to know our names and how we spelled them. I almost tried to act shy but remembered my coaching. I spelled out my name, and the man looked at me so closely I thought something was wrong.

"Miss Josephine, I have to know, are you part Indian?"

I blushed my worst, and Mr. Bigla turned on the man and told him to mind his business.

"No, no, people," the lawyer explained. "I have to know if there is any Indian blood to deal with. If I don't get the paper right the first time, there will not be a second chance in the courts. I'm sorry if I have offended anybody, but I do need to know."

I stammered and said that I was half Indian but was blue-eyed from my white family. The fine gentleman explained to Mr. Bigla that an Indian was not recognized in the courts unless a special note was attached to state the circumstances. I was in a quandary as to my Indian status when the fine man told us that everything was in order.

Spring planting came on the estate in a rush, with extra people cooking outside for the field hands. I wasn't involved except to assist Miss Bessie to see what was going on. She had learned how to get up on her own and use the walker, as we called it. Alex had made her another one that was much lighter, and she could get around well upstairs.

The mayor had another siege of palsy but cleared right up. I met with the doctor from time to time and helped him with difficult cases that didn't seem to heal. All I did was clean them up and their own bodies healed their injuries. The doctor and I exchanged cures; he gave me a medical book that explained the functions of the human body. Some of the pictures were explicit, but I knew they were true and kept those feelings to myself. My face cleared right up except for my temples; there were some marks that were still there. There was a face cream that the white women used to mask wrinkles in their skin. I giggled as I added some brown color to the cream, and we erased those wrinkles on the sides of my eyes.

True to the deal I made with the doctor, I told what I had used to calm my subjects.

"*Sang!* Oh, Miss Josie, there is nothing to those ole herb remedies! How does your recipe work?"

"Doctor, it certainly does work. If you don't believe me, let's go down to the pigpen and I'll show you how." Alex and I escorted him to the pigpen. A pet pig was always out of the pen, and we coached him to eat his portion of Sang with feed. Wasn't long before Mr. Pig was snoring his best. The doctor couldn't believe his eyes. I told Alex that we might as well fix that pig to stay in his pen while he was in la-la land. I neutered that male hog and made him a good tame pig till he was butchered the next fall. Doctor took on anew respect for herbs that day. We went to the house the long way so the doctor could get his respect back and took his leave to the office. Alex and I never told on the doctor, and he in turn had respect for other ways of doctoring.

Life's Changes

Alex and I started dating sometime in the summer as there wasn't anything else to do. We did work on a large estate and had most of our evenings off. At first I was apprehensive in getting close to anyone, but the Lord blessed us with the same temperament, and our romance blossomed. Mr. Bigla gave us his blessings, and the priest married us in a quiet ceremony. We continued to work for the same Mr. and Mrs. Bigla and really enjoyed them. The doctor continued to come by and check on my Miss Bessie. On one of his visits he came to Alex and wanted to drink some tea and talk. We settled into the breakfast nook, and he told us a story we never expected. My Miss Bessie was not going to live much longer; her heart was giving out from the strain of years and lifestyle. The doctor wanted us to try to help the old folks by staying on and seeing them to the end. Alex and I agreed to help them as long as we were needed and then to make our own plans.

With the crops harvested, wood cut for the winter, and butchering complete we had more idle time. For some reason I had been sick in the mornings, and the doctor came to check on Miss Bessie and complimented Alex and me on our coming child.

"No!"

"Yes!" was his final answer. "Congratulations!"

We were awestruck. The Biglas were ecstatic. Alex and I looked at each other and fell into each other's arms.

We suffered through the worst cold spell on record. We used the hired hands to keep the fireplaces going all the time just to keep the chill out. I worked in the kitchen and kept reasonably warm with the wood cookstove and my growing child. My Miss Bessie was back in bed all the time, and her complexion grew so sallow. Alex and I feared the worst and knew we were out of a job as soon as Miss Bessie expired. The doctor did his best, but Miss Bessie soon gave up and waned away. The funeral was a closed-casket ceremony, and we buried her in the family plot on the grounds. Alex and I made our plans to leave, but the doctor begged us to stay awhile longer and take care of Mr. Bigla. We didn't know the rest of the story, and we lost Mr. Bigla in a fortnight. We buried him beside the fresh grave of his wife, in front of all the hired hands, doctor, and the little lawyer we had seen coming and going on business in the study. The lawyer made the announcement that he was the executor of Mr. Bigla's estate. He wanted to see the doctor, Alex, and me in the study the next morning. The lawyer gave me cash money to pay the hired hands off as soon as they had cleaned the house one more time and to tell them they would not be needed anymore. Alex and I made our plans to leave by the next morning and get on with our child rearing.

The lawyer was official the next morning. The doctor was first in line with a very comfortable parting check. He called Alex and me by our full names, then by our married names, then proclaimed the complete estate of Mr. and Mrs. Bigla had been given to us to use as we needed. You could have blown us over with a feather. The doctor congratulated us; the lawyer had us sign the last documents that released him from the estate. The lawyer congratulated us and said he had one last duty to perform: we needed to go to the courthouse to register the deed in our names, and he was to witness the signatures. We all got into a one-horse rig, marched ourselves to the courthouse, and registered the deed. As the lawyer was about to witness the signatures, someone noticed that I was an Indian and pitched the worst fit one could ever hear.

"No, no, no, this cannot be!" was shouted to the four winds. I was ready to fade into the woodwork when the lawyer produced the document, signed by Mr. Bigla, that he recognized me as half Indian and that I could sign an official document. Yes, I was allowed to sign as notarized by the lawyer, and the Bigla estate became ours!

Our Life in Braymer, Missouri

My first child came on the eve of a cool snap, and I had to keep him in the kitchen to stay away from the damps. The doctor came by to check on Linnaeus and noted that I didn't have any kind of a binder on my firstborn. A binder is a strip of cloth wound around babies' stomachs to prevent the navel from protruding.

"W-why," I stammered, "it never occurred to me to bind a healthy baby, Doctor."

"Josie, did your tribe bind their babes?"

"Doctor, I've never seen an Indian baby that had to have a binder of any kind."

"Okay, Miss Josie, let's leave little Linnaeus alone and we'll see what happens."

I could have told him nothing would happen, but I wanted to be nice that day. I furnished enough milk for two babies, but my man-child soon took it all. Alex and I ran an inventory of the whole estate just to see what we had and discovered more than we first thought. I had never walked the forest boundary completely; the deed said we had land that was heavily forested. I knew we had a lot of white oak on the hillside, but the bottom land had huge stands of cottonwood, walnut, and some kind of scrub cedar that was worthless.

The bank sent us a statement, and we had to take all our papers in to get the checking account switched. It was then we were notified that a lock box was in existence. We expected the worst, no, the best—gold! We didn't have a clue until they finally showed us all the legal papers from the past. We scoured them first to see if there was any money—none! Indebtedness— none! Smelly old documents—plenty! We finally gave up on finding any gold and sealed the lock box with our names on the forms. Back at the mansion there had to be a secret room, safe, or something. The Biglas kept detailed records of the farm, and we started noticing that the estate had never made too much money—just a very comfortable living for those two with nothing else. The secret room turned out to be in the cellar, a room completely full of coal, for emergency use only, we surmised. I found a daybook in the study with a series of numbers written on the back page with indelible pencil. I set this aside for future study and continued to turn each book page by page.

I found Miss Bessie's personal book for drying flowers; there must have been a thousand roses all laid out just so. It had the most wonderful smell of dried herbs and roses. I would go back to the daybook for any information of a day-by-day nature. Another account book was for sales of logs, hogs, and cows. Each entry was numbered with that indelible pencil at the end. We started to look for another bank. I had remembered Mr. Bigla traveling to New Orleans once in a while.

We never found another bank; we only found in the daybook more sales for lumber. I got to thinking about lumber, so we found the local mill and asked if Mr. Bigla had sold any logs or had any business with the mill.

"Mr. Alex, if that is your name, it is not any of your business to ask about Mr. Bigla."

Alex explained to the mill operator that Mr. Bigla had died and that we were the heirs of the estate. The operator got on his high horse and demanded a letter from the lawyer that stated that. My Alex pulled out the documents of Mr. Bigla's death, copies of the transferal of the deed, and the paper where I could sign for property.

"Mr. Alex Lorett, it is a pleasure to meet you, and anything you want to know, you ask for Jim Hayrath, owner and operator of this mill."

We got to see the complete operation. I never dreamed that logging was so involved; as it turned out, Mr. Bigla didn't have any trees to be sawn, nor did he owe any money. Oh well, it was a good day's outing for a picnic lunch. Little Linnaeus enjoyed the buggy ride by sleeping the whole way.

Alex hired some help to work the farmland, and I hired Sue back to help with the housework. They were so glad to know they still had a job, and we really needed the help. The farmhouses were all cleaned out and our laborers set up housekeeping. I could just see our family growing and having plenty of kids to play with. Alex and I didn't believe in slaves, so our farm help was just that, hired farm help. We had plenty of hogs to share with the help, and a calf was butchered in the spring for all to use. The garden spot was enlarged to accommodate the extra mouths.

I kept looking for any signs of any missing currency and came back to the day-book inscriptions that eluded me. I found a genealogy book dating back into the 1700s. I looked up the people I knew, found out where all the Biglas were born, including deaths and children. None of it made any impression on me, and I filed it away in its place. How many books there were, I didn't have a clue. There were way too many to count or read. Linnaeus was two by this time, and I was having trouble with morning sickness again. My mornings were a washout. The garden produce had supplied plenty for the farmhands and more to can. I couldn't stand the smell of curing meat, so the butchering was done without me. Alex would come in from the fields bone-tired and was usually asleep by dark each day.

The heat was bad that summer. I spent most of the day away from the kitchen heat. Sue was so good to take over and help me spend the days trying to be comfortable. We had a visitor one day, and he introduced himself as Silas Long, a buyer of logs. His company in New Orleans had sent him up in the Missouri River country to find and float cottonwood logs down to New Orleans to a sawmill that dealt in large logs. He inquired about Mr. Olaf Bigla and wanted to meet with him. I wasn't ready for this visitor, but he did get my interest up when he mentioned Mr. Bigla. We went out to the burial plots, and I showed him the tombstone, as the Biglas' final resting place. The man crossed himself; I went silent to give Silas time to gather himself together. I heard him clear his throat and sob quietly. We walked back to the house. I signaled Sue to make us a cool drink. As we sat on the shady porch, Silas shared with me that he knew the Biglas from his youth and knew Miss Bessie had had a stroke but lost touch with them after that. I shared with him about the last days of my former employers and what they meant to Alex and me.

Alex came by the house and joined us in our cool drink; Silas Long introduced himself to my husband and told him his business. Alex explained to him that the properties had been deeded to us upon their deaths. The papers were brought to him to examine, and he was amazed at the document I had about signing legal papers.

"Mrs. Lorett, I want to apologize. I thought you to be hired help, and I was going to ask for the present owners. I was about to make a huge mistake, but you caught me in midstride and saved the day."

We had a chuckle and invited Silas to join us for the evening meal. He readily accepted and then made the mention that he had stayed with the Biglas for many years while on business.

"Is there a chance that I could rent a room from the Loretts till my journey takes me elsewhere?"

My Alex turned the man down on renting a room but did say it would be a pleasure if he would stay with us. Silas Long smiled and accepted the invitation.

Silas wanted to see the house since we had taken over, and he picked out an upstairs room with an outside porch. He said he couldn't count the times he had slept in that room and pondered life's trials on the porch. We fell into a pattern with Silas not getting up early and taking his time coming to breakfast. Alex was usually gone by the time he came down, and it was up to Sue and me to introduce him to each morning. What a delight to share my time with someone other than my Alex. By the noon meal Silas was fully ready for the rest of the day. They looked at every cottonwood tree on our farm. He made a bid to Alex to move his crew into the groves to cut and transport the logs that he felt would cut the most board feet. His company was only interested in large logs six foot in diameter by twenty feet long. The mill would cut the logs up, and Alex would have to come to New Orleans to check the progress. He would be paid in cash for the board feet at that time. Alex and I did a rough figuring, and the dollar amount was staggering. We signed the papers before Silas could change his mind! We found out then and there where to look for any missing money. One evening we asked Silas what bank Mr. Bigla used when he was in New Orleans, Louisiana.

Mr. Silas Long raised himself up to his full sitting height and stated: "My company is the Bank of New Orleans, and Mr. Bigla's account is currently waiting on my instructions."

We could have drifted off the porch with a breath of air! My Alex, never at a loss for words, said, "Silas, notify us when our logs berth and we will come to your office and get acquainted."

"Yes, yes, that will be the best plan, and we will get all your papers recorded and dutifully notarized for our records," Mr. Silas Long spoke so officially. "Oh, and one more item that is most delicate. Mr. and Mrs. Lorett, we have a direct mandate from the United States Government not to have any dealings with Indians. I think at this time we should have Mrs. Lorett wear a veil till we get into our offices."

I spoke up with a most distinct voice, "Mr. Silas Long, I will come with white powder all over my face and a long white veil if that will get the job done." I did okay until I had to snicker, then we all laughed at the situation.

"Mrs. Josephine Lorett, in all honesty, I have never seen an Indian woman so beautiful in all my life."

I tried not to blush and thanked the little ole man with all my heart.

The men came with all the necessary equipment to log the cottonwood. I couldn't imagine what size equipment would be needed to haul the timber to the Missouri River, much less to saw all of it into usable pieces. One day all that equipment went by our house headed for its watery journey to New Orleans. I delivered a hefty man-child that night, whom we named Lawrence.

The Bank of New Orleans sent us a letter upon Mr. Slias Long's return to the coast, welcoming us as bank depositors. They gave us a list of legal papers to bring, and we would be furnished living quarters during our business with the Bank of New Orleans. We toyed with the idea of going overland to New Orleans, but we wanted to ride the steam-powered *River Queen* that plied the Mississippi to New Orleans. We took Sue with us as nanny and made a gala affair of planning to get on the water as soon as we were notified our logs were at the mill. The official notice came while northern Missouri was still in the grip of cold spring rains. We had to bundle up for the overland ride in a covered surrey for those thirty miles to the Missouri River. Oh, of all the noise and traffic at the Camden Bend landing, our horses were well-mannered, but this was a might much.

We boarded the *River Queen* one afternoon and were to embark the next morning at daylight. Our accommodations were just below the pilot house, and we had a clear view of the whole river. The captain gathered all the passengers in the dining room that evening for a sumptuous meal and introduction to river travel. We tried to keep our small group in sight all the time and were nervous about being separated. I felt the *River Queen* slip out in the current just as the sun made its appearance, and I hit the deck, wanting to see the world slip by. I was so captivated by all the goings-on that I never noticed my Alex till it was too late. He was hung over the fantail, as they called the rear end of the *River Queen, feeding the fish!* Oh, he lost all he had eaten for a month and then some. Me? Never a qualm's feeling.

We traveled by the daylight hours and looked forward to tying up to the bank at night. There was always a group of men waiting to tie us up and almost immediately replenished the wood burnt in the boiler.

This became the norm for the trip down the Missouri. The captain told us that as soon as we plied our way to the Mississippi, we could travel at night too. My Alex fought each morning with the seasickness but gradually learned to get up before daylight, have breakfast, and enjoy the morning cool.

One morning I awoke to dead silence; not one soul was stirring. I awoke Alex, and he listened. Only our captain was walking the deck, trying to look through the fog! We stayed moored till midmorning, and soon river traffic was restored. Of all the hooting and tooting I had ever heard, it came from the river traffic. Alex finally figured out we were traveling by sound only!

Plying the Mississippi

As we slipped out in the Mississippi River, we could feel the *River Queen* speed up. The river was wider than a mile across. Our forward progress took us right out to the center of the river, and a huge boat that was black with soot came abreast of us. They came closer, and I reckoned that we were going to smack together. The deck hands gathered at the bow and the stern and threw ropes back and forth to each other. It seemed so strange that both boats came together so gently, becoming as one plying the water to New Orleans together. The deckhands got out a set of large troughs and started shoveling coal into the coal bins on the *River Queen*. I don't know how much weight the *River Queen* took on as we settled in the water. The captain went over the gangplank, paid the bill, and I think he stayed too long because he smelled of rot gut whisky when he staggered back aboard. The parting of boats was so simple; the ropes were thrown back, and the *River Queen* never stopped or hesitated. Our meal that evening was without our captain.

As the days warmed up, we spent more time on the deck. One of the deckhands came one day with a line; it looked like a rope to me and was strung out like a clothesline. Then he snapped a hook on the line and gave me the loose end. I wondered what in the world it was for. He soon returned with a harness the size of our Linnaeus. He helped me fit it on the yard runner, tied my loose end to the harness, and we let that tyke have the run of the deckhouse. You have never seen such carrying on by somebody let loose. We didn't have to hold him all the time. The same man came back and signed, "What is the boy's name?"

"Oh, that name is much too long. Let's call him Lin."

I agreed, and we called Linnaeus Lin for the rest of the trip.

"Hey You" brought a toy that had wheels, and Lin could make all those noises of the *River Queen*. I tried to talk to the man, but he spoke another language that I didn't know and he had a dark complexion. I asked the captain, and he said he was a Cajun mix.

"Hey You!" was called, and the man started talking that Cajun slang. We talked up a storm; no, we both signed at once. The captain told Hey You to go do something then turned to me and said, "Ma'am, you don't have to talk to Hey You. He is just a deckhand, can't read or write."

I looked him in the eye and told Mr. Uppity-up that Hey You was a human being and I wanted to talk to him.

"Ma'am, you misunderstand me. Hey You is just a Cajun deckhand, and you don't have to talk to him."

I tried to talk to the captain but to no avail; maybe I would try again at a later date.

We spent the next month on the *River Queen,* with each day bringing us closer to our destination. Missouri was cold and wet when we left, but Mississippi was just wet. We could plan on rain each day just after the noon meal. Lin liked to play in the sun, and I found out I couldn't stay out too long. Boy, did my face get hot. I made a note not to get too much sun, just like the doctor said. Sue, Linnaeus, and Lawrence became good friends, and I was glad to have the help.

Our date with the coal tenders was kept every few days, and we made good time going with the current. Alex and the deckhands kept us in catfish caught off the side of the *River Queen.* We ate fish so many different ways, and did we love it. As we got closer to New Orleans, the captain told us we were going to get seafood from an old scowl they called a fishing boat. Alex and I couldn't figure out how the captain would get the service boats to come alongside until the shrimp boat. A new flag was run up by lanyard that had a picture of a shrimp. They tied up to us as we made way, and the cook and a helper took their tubs over and came back with crawdad-looking creatures. My Alex took on a green pallor and said, "Josie, I can't eat something that looks like a bug!" I didn't have a clue what was going to be cooked, but the smell sold me.

We got Alex to supper, and the captain showed us how to peel the rind, dip them in horseradish, and we dined on the first seafood of the trip. The cook fixed some kind of flat turtle-looking seashell they called crabs. I got one whiff of a creature that smelled to high heavens; I passed that to the next person!

Our seafood dinners were limited to shrimp, tuna,

red fish, all kinds of oysters, and we gradually took a liking to fish of all kinds. We even took a liking to red beans and rice. What we enjoyed the most was we didn't have to catch or cook the meals. Traffic seemed to multiply as we got closer to New Orleans. The captain told us to stay in the center of the *River Queen,* for we might get bumped. We took on our last load of coal the next evening and bedded down early.

New Orleans

We slipped into our berth during the night so quiet, all us landlubbers slept through the whole thing. Alex and I woke right at the crack of dawn and slipped out onto the deck to an all-new world. Unloading started as soon as the black men arrived with their two-wheeled dollies. Hey You, was the man for the job; he could speak their language, sing the songs, and the unloading of the *Queen* went off without a hitch. I was so engrossed with the unloading that Mr. Silas Long came aboard without us noticing. His first remark was, "If all you gawking landlubbers would care to come with me, we will have breakfast on the dock."

We laughed and scampered down the gangplank into New Orleans. Silas took us on a tour of the town in one of those white rigs that were such a delight to ride in, and we spent the first day like he said, "gawking." The next day I wore my long white veil and met with the lawyers, and officials of the Bank of New Orleans and signed our names into all the records. A snack in Boardwalk Café was a relief for all involved.

They took me back to the rooming house, and we took our afternoon nap as Silas and Alex went with a guide and verified the right number of logs with his name painted on the ends. They were to be sawn the next morning, first in line. Alex and I could hardly sleep that night in our assigned bed and breakfast. Sue kept the boys the next day, and our guided tour of the sawmill started in a raised house next to the mill pond. Our logs could be seen in the races, ready to start the first run. Of all the steam making its hissing, the clouds of moisture, and the whistles telling the mill to start the day, we were again caught with our mouths open! The first log went through the saw with nothing but a hissing sound, and a slab fell off on the track the size of a small canoe. Then more went through till the six-foot-by-twenty-foot behemoth was no more. All this went inside to be cut into smaller sizes and came out on a rail car, cut, banded, and ready to ship off to a furniture factory.

Our logs were to be kiln dried, cut to even smaller sizes, and covered with soft padding to make furniture for the world. Alex and I stayed till the whole run, with our names on the end, was cut and on the rail-cars. Silas came and picked us up for the noon meal and an appointment with the bank officials. We wondered what could top the sawn logs with our names on the end. Lunch was a Cajun dish prepared by a French chef. Silas did all the ordering, and we got our first spicy Cajun meal!

Our trip back to the bank was by one of those white carriages, and we all tried to talk at the same time. We met with the acquisitions officer, and he had not been filled in about a white man with an Indian wife. I just knew that the deal was to be called off; we would be left with a million wet boards to be shipped back to our tree farm in Missouri! Silas Long stepped up to the task and explained that all our papers were in order and on file in the bank vaults. The officer explained that he had to make sure because he could lose his job if the papers weren't made out right. After some tense moments, the papers were produced and a check was drawn on the Bank of New Orleans for our logs. Alex and I saw the check and blanched with the thought of trying to carry all that money back with us. Silas Long came to our rescue again and explained that Mr. Bigla had always deposited his log sales into the bank and the amount transferred to his bank in Braymer, Missouri. Oh yes, the bank account of Mr. Bigla.

Alex and I asked as one, "How much money is in that account?" The acquisition officer and Silas both scratched their heads, and finally we all came up with the same answer. All of us had forgotten about Mr. Bigla's banking account. We had to do all the business of transferal into our names and records. We found the old account balance was zero; Mr. Bigla's balance had been transferred to the Bank in Braymer, Missouri. Our account balance swelled with the latest sale.

Silas Long said we had one last item of business to conduct with the president of the bank. We met in the most spacious office in the building, and the kind Mr. Swak shook both our hands and said, "Mrs. Josephine Lorett, I want you to take your veil off and show you to my wife." His wife of many years came into the room, and I about gulped out loud. The woman was the same brown color as me. She held her head up high and spoke with correct Oxford English.

"Mrs. Josephine Lorett, the stories of your beauty have proceeded you to our humble business. I want to compliment you for staying the course through all this transferal of business of names and legalities. I too have had trouble with being an Indian woman who could sign my own papers. I see you have had a very good lawyer and have gotten the right papers to conduct business. The reason I called a meeting with you is to inform all that are involved that the United States Government has a bill on the floor of the Senate that will again strip all Indians of any rights to sign their own business papers."

I could see all those papers. I asked, "What can be done?"

"Okay, Mr. and Mrs. Alex Lorett, this is what my husband and I have done. We have drawn up papers that give my husband complete control over my part of the business."

I thought to myself, *I know now who owns the bank.*

"If I were you, Mrs. Lorett, before you leave the bank, I would draw up a complete set of papers and date them today to give Mr. Alex Lorett the powers to conduct business in your absence."

I wanted to talk with my Alex, and we went into another office and agreed to get the papers drawn up and dated that day. The bank lawyer came and got the right names. He already had the papers drawn up, we signed them, and then we went back to the *River Queen*.

River Queen

The return trip to Braymer, Missouri, was a complete reversal, except we were carrying staples in wooden barrels. The whole boat smelled of spices, and I remembered the herbs that were cured in my little shed. I got my fill of those staples and took my turn on the fantail feeding the fish every morning of the return trip. If I could just get off the boat! Of course, it took us longer. That Mississippi going upstream was hard and dangerous. The coal boats came each time that flag with a picture of a piece of coal was flown. Hey You, was the man of the hour each time and spouted instructions like a sailor. I didn't have a clue what was being said, but the work was done in record time. I felt sorry for the *River Queen* having to *chug chug* twice as hard going upstream.

The cook bought all kinds of food right over the side of the service boats. One day a long, sleek boat came alongside, and we immediately smelled pineap-

ples and saw every kind of fruit that grows in southern
Louisiana. They stocked several holds and completely
filled each hold with chipped ice until the cover sat
askew. Seafood came aboard the next boat, then more
ice on top of the fish. Fresh water, chunk ice, sacks of
dried beans, corn, all kinds of fresh ear corn, tomatoes,
and potatoes by the bin full. We asked the captain why
we were taking on so much food, and he explained we
were stocking enough to get us into Camden Landing,
Missouri. We forgot we were headed home.

We left the mosquito-infested swamps of southern
Louisiana and got back to the reality of being inland.
The *River Queen* hove Arkansas into view one afternoon, and I wished we could have watched the land-
scape slip by all night long. We had two more states
of traveling on the Mississippi for me to reflect on our
travels. We didn't have a chance to have mass on the
trip, so I would silently sit in the evenings with my
family by my side, and I would pray my prayer beads
completely around. I really thought my religion was
completely hidden from the hands of the boat until the
captain called Alex and me to the wheelhouse.

As he started in, he took his hat off and apologized
for making such a fuss about me talking to Hey You.

"Miss Josie, I'm sorry for talking to you like I did.
The hands on the *River Queen* are all Cajun bred, and,
as you said, they are people too. Yes, I understand what
you were talking about now, and I want to tell you and
Alex what has happened since you have been with us
all these months."

*What in the world have we done? Will they put us off
on some foreign land?* I thought.

"Captain, please tell us what is going on."

"Mr. and Mrs. Alex Lorett, you have been Christian witnesses to my crew each evening on my boat without even knowing it. You sit down with your family and have late-afternoon prayers just before the evening meal. Have you watched my crew take their hats off? Did you notice how quiet they become while you're praying? Have you seen them cross themselves when you're through? I'm ashamed to say it, but we have never had mass on the *River Queen*."

Alex let the captain compose himself and proposed we let the prayer time be a witness to the boat crew. We left the wheelhouse that evening and gathered in the galley hall for supper, and wouldn't you know it, the captain called on Alex to bless the food.

I slipped a look around and was so proud of all those rough deckhands with their hats in their hands and crossing themselves at the last amen.

We plied into Arkansas that night with full hearts, thanking the Lord for using us to witness to another race of people. Our trip through Arkansas laid out the finest of the trip. We could see the spring-summer taking over the land. Crops had been planted in the bottoms, and we could see down the rows of corn. We traveled through the deer lands we had heard of and saw many fawns springing their way around nervous does. They shouldn't have worried; we were on our way to Camden Landing, Missouri, as fast as our *River Queen* could chug! I lost track of the times the coal tenders came alongside as we matched their speed. The last fill-up, the hands brought out planks and fenced the coal bins off and loaded us with as much of those messy black rocks as would stay on deck. The captain called us to the stateroom and explained that we were taking on extra coal to get us up into the Missouri River. There had been a large spring storm, and we were going to go up the Mississippi, drop anchor, and ride out the high waters.

Our first sight was flotsam from a shipwreck down the center of the river; trees, stumps, cattle, and then acres of trash came on the river. The captain took us on the lee side, and we slid around the inlet of the Missouri into the eddy waters of the mighty Mississippi.

Missouri

The boat hands let a huge anchor out on each end of the *River Queen,* and we rode out the flood about a half-mile upstream. We could watch the flood and were glad we could stay away. Our anchorage was away from the bank; this kept us out of harm's way from the river bandits that prowled the banks day and night. Hey You, and others took their turns for and aft with some big blunder busts called shotguns. They said they would raise the dead. I didn't want any part of the river bandits! Hey You, clotheslined Lin in the center of the deck again, and was he was a happy boy! I think that was one of the best things that could happen during our trip. The Mississippi River always had rain sometime during the day, and Lin got to where he would play in the rain while onboard.

The captain was always on the lookout for anything abnormal, and one lazy afternoon while we were trying to take a nap, we heard this *a-ca-boom* from one of the blunder bust's shotguns. *A-ca-boom!* from the other end of the *Queen* put us underway. I just knew they did that on purpose to wake us up for the sight of getting started into the Missouri River. They had gotten up a full head of steam as the *River Queen* fairly scooted downriver to get lined up with the main channel of our Missouri River. We slowed down as the river caught us, and we crept upstream ever so slowly. I had shut my eyes, thinking that would help us make way. It must have, as I felt the *Queen* gather speed. That ole thing was belching so much smoke, it fair made a haze all over. We stayed close to the center going upriver because of the trash on the sides. We were using way too much coal, and I had visions of floating back out into the Mississippi, when we spied the cords of wood stacked up on the bank. We slipped sideways, and the catch men tied us up to a huge tree on the bank. The gangplank was a highway for the men and the wheelbarrows full of wood. We soon tired of all the activity and supped with the captain till it was bedtime. Our instructions for tomorrow: tie everyone down real good. We were in for a blow and possible rough waters.

We got our fill of rough waters just after breakfast. As the day wore down, the wind took its leave, and we spent the night along the banks taking on more wood. I tried to write down each day, but the days became what we called sameness. There was absolutely no change from day to day: eat, sleep, talk to the deckhands, get fat and lazy!

Fat? Yes, I mean too big, eat too much prepared food, too little exercise. My Alex could hardly button his pants, and for sure he couldn't tie his shoes. I was slim and trim, wore my dresses with ease, and nursed my Lawrence; that chubby was a lapful. Sue had gained her share of weight and mumbled about how bad the food tasted. I grew impatient, was tired all the time, and griped about how the food smelled. The captain shouted too much; the deckhands swore in their language. I don't know who got the gripe first, but we were a boatload of sick, sorry-looking human beings. It was up to the first mate to get steam up enough to go upstream. The sorry attempts to make headway found us all over the river. As the saying goes, all things will pass in time, and we lost three days tied up on the banks of the Missouri River. We finally got over whatever we had and made some progress north. Alex was much slimmer. I was peaked, the crew was weak as kittens, and we sailed into Camden Landing. How long we plied the Missouri River from south to north was way too long. We were so anxious to get home.

If it was possible, Camden Landing was even noisier than before. We arrived at the busiest time of the day, and the captain told us we would have to wait our turn before docking. I thought, *No, no. If I have to stay any longer, I will have seasickness.* We slept so fitfully that night but must have gone off asleep because we were tied up the next morning and about one-half unloaded when we got our breakfast. Miracles happened that morning. I was able to keep my biscuits and gravy down. We hired a surrey and spent the whole day getting home. I didn't care how rough the road was; I just wanted to get home to my easy chair. We were so tired and cross by the time the night lights told us that we had arrived. We sat down and looked at each other and slept awhile in our misery.

The field hands had taken care of planting of our huge garden, Alex had to make a trip to the bank to make sure of the transfer of our funds, and I knew there was trouble when he came back with the horses lathered.

"Josie, come quick! We have to get back to the bank with all our papers and make sure they are all in order."

The lawyer was there when we arrived and had the attention of the bank president. They told all that was going on; we only had a few days to transfer all my business into Alex's name. We signed the papers, and the lawyer said he was going to the county seat to register the documents; he would come out to the farm the next day and give us our news. We spent another fitful night, but the lawyer came for breakfast the next morning with the papers and said we just made it. There was a big hubbub in all the state because of what the United States was doing to the Indians. I just wanted to hide my face but remembered the banker's wife, how she held her head up high and went on with life.

Alex and hands took some logs to our local mill and had them cut so we could build another barn. They hauled the rough-sawn lumber and stored it in a curing shed. Alex, ever the carpenter, spent some time building us a smokehouse before butchering time. I was able to help with the hogs and saw the possibility of meat for all the hands and some besides as we butchered eight fat ones. Oh, the work we got into that fall, curing, stuffing sausages, making head cheese, pickling pigs' feet, then before we quit for the winter we killed a small calf so everybody could have a good mess of beef.

We began to hear all kinds of stories about the lands that were going to open up for settlement in Indian Territory. Alex would come in from town and be so depressed with the way they were displacing the Indians.

"Why, I hear they are driving them like cattle into Indian Territory and just making them live off the land!" He didn't know the way I was treated, and one night I told him the whole story of what I had gone through just so I could be here now. Alex cried through his hands then held me so tenderly and said, "Josie, I will never let them harm you anymore. Let's move out into Indian Territory and disappear!"

That wasn't what I wanted to hear, but I kept his sayings close to my heart. We made a pact that day that if things got bad we would do just that.

The times came and went with the turmoil getting worse daily; I had to go to town one day and never thought much about it. I did my trading and was headed home when I saw the militia gathering Indians by the score for transport west. My horse outran that mob, and I hid in the barn while Alex confronted the sergeant in charge. I couldn't hear what was being said but did know it was about me. Alex took the sergeant inside and showed him the paper we had signed. This seemed to satisfy all concerned, and they left in a huff because of losing another Indian. Alex found me hiding under a pile of straw, crying my eyes out, and we knew the days were numbered for our trip to Indian Territory. It was in the night when I realized we had company; the field hands' dogs had treed something in the barn. A lamp was lit, and we searched the grounds around the barn. Some ole mutt treed up the ladder to the hayloft. Alex had brought a gun and was ready to blow a hole the size of my thumb through something when we heard someone say, "Please don't shoot. I'm not armed." An ole scruffy man came down the ladder so slowly.

I know that shuffle, I thought. The man turned out to be the doctor! *What is our world coming to? A man educated to be a doctor hiding in our hayloft.*

We took the doctor into our house and fed him first. Alex gave him a bath, and it was then we noticed the whip marks all over his brown Indian skin. I spread soothing ointment from my plant stock, as Alex dressed him in some small clothes. I made tea and made sure he got a portion of sang; it was as if a weight had been taken off his shoulders as we put him to bed, clothes and all. I checked on him before daylight and found him full of fever. Alex and I spread some more of that soothing gel and left him to his slumber. This went on for two days, as his fever gradually went down and we got more and more food down him. The third morning we had our visitor join us for breakfast. As the story unfolded, he had been rounded up with the rest of the Indians and was being sent to Indian Territory. He had escaped, made his way back to Braymer, and thought about our estate being close by. We welcomed him and told about our own plans to move to the Territory. Our doctor joined the plans to do just that.

It was soon apparent we needed to call the doctor something besides Doctor. We tried several names, but nothing came out for sure. We discussed options, and then we remembered that the militia was only hunting brown Indians. Then the thought came that if Alex had hired hands that were black, the militia wouldn't bother us. We had some former slaves who were black as night, and if Doc and I could change our color, we had the problem solved. We named the doctor Boy! The problem with the color came from an old recipe for tanning animal hides. I had a bucket of green walnut shells brought up from the tree farm and made my own stain. I let them steep in the juices and rubbed them on our feet! We turned the best ebony color you have ever seen; even washing with lye soap wouldn't take that off.

Boy and I had a plan to hide ourselves in plain sight of the militia, and they wouldn't know the difference. Now for clothes. What could I make to look like common field workers? The answer came from the former slaves we had hired as full-time help. I explained that we wanted to disguise ourselves to appear as field hands. Our complete camp got into the act of fooling the militia! First a change of dress, with apron and hair wrap for me. Boy was given a used set of overalls stained with cotton stalk juice. I stained all our exposed flesh that ebony color, and Alex and our help about split their lips laughing. Then they rubbed our stained flesh to see if any of the color would come off! The final lesson in language was provided by our help. They had us practice saying a few slang words, calling each other Boy and Sister. We could hardly keep a straight face from all the laughin'.

Our change into field hands came over night, and Boy and I felt we could pull it off. Our plans began to grow as to when we would strike out to Indian Territory. Alex bought mules aplenty to move two large wagons one hooked to the other. Alex fed the mules out of the back of the wagons, and it really helped while on our way. Wherever we were, there came the thundering herd at feeding time. I never grew tired of watching the flashing bodies of horse flesh. All our farm machinery completely filled the back wagon, with some tied on the sides and room for hay and grain. We made the front wagon our living quarters with high bows and a large sailcloth cover to keep out of the elements.

Trailing to Oklahoma, 1891

We closed up the estate and said good-bye to all the hands that spring. Alex had them stay as long as they wanted just to watch the place. Boy and I made our transition to hired help overnight and made the best of the situation. Alex was to be the main spokesman; Boy and I were to keep our mouths shut and hope for the best. Our first day out was a fiasco: the mules wouldn't behave; we couldn't seem to get those ornery four-legged beasts to pull together. Alex saddled up his horse and got out a black snake whip, about twelve feet long. All he did was crack it a couple of times each morning and we had well-mannered mules the whole day.

We headed for the Kansas line as directly as we could. We had heard that there were a lot of Plains Indians out on the tall grass prairie, and I knew their sign language. Four miles that first day was plenty to put the tired on man and beast. Alex and Boy hobbled the horses and let the rest forage on their own. We fried bacon over a wood fire with sourdough bread and milk. Our milk cow, Jerz, became my charge, as she was so gentle I could milk her anywhere and had plenty of warm milk to drink. The boys thought we were on a permanent outing, but we turned in early under the wagons. Before daylight all the running stock did just that; they would wake up the dead as they stormed the back of the wagon for their daily ration. I stoked the fire alive and made oatmeal with warm milk from Jerz. We slicked the pot clean and got on the road right after a couple of cracks from that black snake. Those mules had to be reminded who was boss every morning. We all took turns riding on the horses and could see much more of the country. I even took my turn riding the chuck wagon. The trees were thick and close to the trail; we all wondered how many outlaws had ridden the trail to Kansas.

Our first contact with another wagon was a crossroad going to Camden Landing. Boy and I almost blew our cover, but we looked embarrassed and had to hide our heads to keep from smiling. Alex took over the visiting and talked about the weather and getting back on the trail. I had packed plenty of jelly for us a noon snack, and we ate on the trail without stopping. We lost track of the miles in the forest and agreed it didn't make sense to keep track of the miles anyway. Alex was headed to Atchison to take a ferry across the Missouri River; I worried about our cover and kept dobbing any light area that shone on Boy and me. We shouldn't have worried, we could shut our mouths at night, and nobody could have found us.

The second night we camped by a large spring with another set of wagons going, where else, but to Indian

Territory. Boy and I assumed our cover and let the menfolk do all the talking. The guests always referred to us as the hired help. I was used to being quiet, but Boy let his education slip a time or two with some remark about a medical point. Alex took over and had Boy tell them what the cure for infected tongue was. Boy, always one with a quick answer, pulled himself up to the top of his five-foot-two and said, "That question is so simple I will let my nurse answer."

I blanched at the thought and looked so perplexed and answered simply, "Quit licking the cat and keep your mouth shut!"

The camp exploded with laughter, and this broke the ice. Slim and Nella and their twin boys looked over the subterfuge. The decision was to travel together, and we felt much safer on the way to my own home.

The trip through the forest of west Missouri is flecked with hills, rocks, very little dirt, and we all got tired of not seeing anything but trees. Alex, always one to travel early in the mornings, was fraught with wet! I had never gotten into such a soggy mess with wet vegetation. There was no way I could get a fire started with wet wood, much less keep the dirt out of our food. Boy and I (the hired hands!) always tried to be clean with food. We changed the first meal of the day to bread and jam, much to the delight of the four boys. This put us on the trail much sooner in the morning. Alex and the boys would ride the horses two at a time and scout ahead for a long stop for lunch. Nella and I rode together, and we wore out our jaws visiting. Oh, the stories we told. This put Nella sitting on the wagon seats with me, and she discovered my dark make-up.

I've goofed, I thought. Boy and I will be discovered.

"Josephine, you are trying to be somebody you're not. What is going on?"

I stammered and really tried to tell her as she intercepted my telling.

"Josephine, you don't have to tell me anything you don't want to. Let's forget what I asked and we'll be friends."

"Nella, I will tell you in time about the make-up, but we need to get into Kansas as soon as we can. I don't want to put you and Slim in harm's way."

Our lunch was a gala affair with both families putting our food together and the boys playing amongst the trees. While the boys were down for a nap, the two families agreed that as soon as we reached Kansas, we would strike due south and try to travel in the grasslands.

That day we noticed wagons all headed west to St. Joseph Landing across the Missouri. There didn't seem any end of the squeaking wheels headed to a new land. We had a meeting with Slim and Nella. We would take the longest way to Atchison, Kansas, and maybe the wagons wouldn't be in such a press. Our daily progress grew as we trail hardened along with the stock. A layover on the Platte River replenished our sourdough bread, washed our sodden clothes, and dried them on the sand plum bushes. The menfolk backed the wagons down in the water, and we hand-scrubbed our trail smell down the river. Slim broke out his fishing equipment and soon had all the boys catching bullheads. We ate like kings that night: fresh fried catfish, sourdough bread, warm milk from Jerz, and the very best was clean bodies inside clean clothes! We filled all the water barrels, as we had a long trek the next two days until we would get to the Missouri River.

The next day we started before daylight, as we felt there was going to be trouble. Boy put a heavy hand on the lines and we started out. Slim had the first trouble with Alex having to crack his black snake a couple of times, and we soon wore down the mules enough to move along. The next problem came in the form of a coyote moving along with the cows; a sharp snap of the black snake soon put him over the ridge. It was some time in the morning when the militia showed up in force and our stealth training took over. Slim and Alex let them inspect our wagons. Boy and I kept quiet. The sergeant in charge seemed to be satisfied and made a show of leaving and then came charging to the wagon holding Boy and me! We were petrified but held our ground in the wagon seat.

Sternly, Boy spoke in his best southern drawl, "What you'll want heah?"

The troop left in a two-by-two column, laughing their best.

If that's what it takes to get to the territory, we thought, *let them laugh!*

Our dinner turned into a victory celebration of fooling the militia. Slim and Nella just shook their heads, wondering what we were trying to do. I had to bite my tongue to keep my secret.

The day smoothed out with an opening of the trees to let the sun's lights come in. We made good time until the stock got to snatching the tall turkey foot grass, as we called it, and Alex stopped right at dark to the relief of both families. The pulling stock just got out from under the harness before they started filling their bellies with that grass. I milked Jerz before she got away, as we made a dry camp that night and fed the families with that good sourdough bread and a big jar of peach jam. The boys drank their fill of milk just before they made it under the wagon to sleep. The coyote had the last laugh that night, but we only heard one yelp. We were wakened the next morning as usual with the thundering herd. Alex got up to rub his stock and found another horse with ours. We didn't have a clue where it came from until I noticed it was an Indian's horse. I got a short piece of rope and made a bridle; whoa, that horse was trained to ride barebacked. Slim and Nella were amazed that I could ride a saddled horse, much less barebacked.

We got on the trail after a quick lick of jelly and a promise of a good dinner. I rode my steed around the country some and noticed Indian sign on the high plateaus. I found the steed's rider in form of an old man, cold as death. I listened for a heartbeat and went for Boy to help me. He tried to revive the old brave, but he had stopped breathing in the night. We set him up on an above-ground shelf, and we gave him the way to the Promised Land of the Indians. Boy and I went back to the wagons, and as we stepped up I noticed the first of the great birds with the red necks circling. Slim and Nella had never seen what was going on, and I made another note to tell all as soon as we got into Kansas.

The Missouri River showed itself to us with all its plunder riding the waves. We had seen the river at flood stage in the summer of '86 when riding the Mississippi. The river ferry was on the other side of the river smoking up Kansas. As the ferry plied itself to the Missouri side, I wished we had gone to St. Louis. That ole tub was soot on all over, and we were going to ride its deck. Alex had been working with our mules on crossing water, but that tub put the whoa to the whole string. The sailors had been there before; they ran out a bull rope connected to the front wagon and then very gently pulled wagons, mules, and all on the boat. I had to take back my thoughts about the pretty little boat. Slim and Nella's rig came on the same way as we herded the walking stock into a pen on the back. As we launched into the deep, the ferry made its *chug chug* sounds at all the right times, and we missed the trees and trash coming down the waters of the Missouri.

The hour it took to get across was filled with a lot of "lookie theres." The captain settled up with Alex and Slim before we got across; his only job was to press the boat up against the west bank, and we tripped right out into Kansas. We had asked where the best place to camp for the night was, and the captain told us about the Stranger River just out of Atchison. They warned us about a camp of Plains Indians that was in the area and to watch our stock real close. We got on the trail, much to the relief of the stock; that ferry had made all of us jelly-legged.

The Hawk

True to the predictions of the captain, I saw those cone-shaped teepees in the distance. I changed into my buckskins and rode my found steed very carefully to the largest teepee, which should have belonged to the chief. As I grew near, several braves met me on the outside and spoke an unknown language. I signed back as they looked over the stud. They couldn't believe that a black woman was returning their horse. The old chief came out and rubbed his horse all over and spoke their language to his staff. Almost immediately the chief's squaw came out and signed for me to get down and seat myself by her fire. I kept my head bowed where they couldn't see my blue eyes and waited for them to decide what to do. The woman explained that her name was White Feather and asked what they should call me. I respectfully signed that I didn't have an Indian name, but she could call me Raven's Girl. I could see the wonder in White Feather's face, and she went about getting me something to drink and eat.

Little did I know what talk was going on outside the teepee until the elders filed in. I had ridden right into an Indian camp of the Plains Indians and was seated with the elders. White Feather spoke to The Hawk and gave him my name of Raven's Girl. All eyes bore a hole right throguh the air to me, and I was almost fearful of my well-being. Maybe I had made a mistake riding in on an unknown stud. The questions came signed about as to why I was riding The Hawk's horse. I explained about the horse coming in with our mules, and I had been riding him from across the river. I told him about finding an old dead brave and putting him on an above-ground platform and telling him to go on to his reward. I could see several nods of approval. The Hawk came back and thanked me for burying the old man, bringing his horse back, and now he wanted to know why I was looking like a black woman with Indian blood in my veins. I told the whole story of why the militia was putting all the Indians in the Territory, how they were making them starve to death, and that I was going there with my white husband. I got several nods of approval, and all the elders left me with The Hawk and his squaw, White Feather. The Hawk spoke about Raven, how he had heard the stories of her healing power, and asked if I was a healer.

"Yes, but not as good as Raven. She was teaching me when she died. The tribe had burnt her inside her teepee with all her herbs. I searched her teepee after the tribe left and buried her skull in a sand bank. Then I left never to go back to the Indian way of life again."

The Hawk rose and led me outside of his teepee. There was the stud I had rode, with a decorated bridle and saddle blanket. The Hawk took the stud by the bridle and signed for me to get on the horse. He gave me the reins and signed, "I give you my horse for being so honest." White Feather came with a lap robe and signed that I had the most beautiful blue eyes she had ever seen. White Feather gave me a soap plant and told me to wash in the Stranger River, for it would take the black off me.

I made my trail back to camp and was greeted by our family of boys. I hugged them and told them their mother had been on a trip to the Indian village and that all was well. Nella and I went down to the Stranger River, and I washed myself, clothes and all, at the same time. The soap plant had done its job when I saw Nella smile. I sent all the menfolk to do the same thing while we made an old-fashioned supper of fried sourdough bread, bacon, and fresh milk. Doc and I changed back into our regular clothes, and we spent the whole evening telling our tale of fooling the militia in Missouri.

Kansas Prairie Mass

Alex said early mass that morning on the Kansas prairie. I put my crucifix on the hub of the wagon, took my string of beads, and said the prayers. We all stood and said amen in unison. Everybody seemed at peace with God as we started south to my own home. The sassafras trees opened up as we came over the Missouri River, none to soon for us. Grass could be had for all the stock by grabbing mouthfuls while traveling. We kept the Stranger River in sight on our left and made the best of time coming over the big rivers. We found a trading post at Potter, and we decided to spend some time resting the stock and ourselves. Doc said he would keep the camp if we would all go in and enjoy ourselves. Yes, just what we needed to replenish our supplies.

Nella and I made the Potter Trading Post while Slim and Alex visited with the blacksmith. We giggled like two school girls while filling our shopping list, entertaining the storekeeper, his sweet wife, and three towheaded girls. I thought we should keep those girls in mind, for they just might like to talk to my boys in time.

We finished our list as the men came charging up to the post at breakneck speed. They grabbed our supplies, and we found out that a renegade bunch was making the rounds. We made the dust fly all the way back and could see dust coming from our camp, men circling and shouting. Slim got his Sharps 50cal. and let off several rounds, and the dust followed the fleeing bunch over the hill. Doc came out of the lead wagon at a run and said we had causalities. My Owl Dung was gone, and one of the calves had a bullet through the neck and was bleeding really bad. The report of my horse being gone devastated me. I figured out if somebody tried to ride him, that old robber was going to have the surprise of his life. Doc and I tried to help the calf, but he was almost bled out. A well-aimed shot from Alex put the poor beast out of his misery.

All four of the boys witnessed the trail law: Do what you have to do and go on with the drive. We dined on beef that night, fried in bacon grease in an open cast-iron pan. The boys all said they couldn't eat that calf. Nella made gravy in the same pan with the meat. We noticed they sopped the pan clean with sourdough bread! The menfolk dressed the rest of the calf, hand-rubbing it with salt and pepper. I boiled the calf in the big iron Dutch oven all night long. By daylight the night-cooled pan was covered and stored in the back of the cook wagon so we could get to it at noon the next day.

We stored all our goods in the wagons and made plans to get on the trail south at daylight. I yearned for Owl Dung, but my stud was not to be seen. Alex didn't have to snap his black snake anymore; the mules had given up on making a fuss as long as they got their morning ration of grain. Slim would hand-rub them, and they gentled down just like horses.

The land was rolling by then, and we couldn't see a thing, but then we could see from horizon to horizon from the tops of the hills. We had stopped for the noon meal for the young calf with plenty of butter on bread. I looked into the Dutch oven and muttered, "This bunch will have to have a rabbit or two to have enough for supper." The boys were tuckered out from the early start, and we all took an afternoon nap in the shade of a big cottonwood tree.

The commotion started over the knoll, and the menfolk strained their eyes to see what was going on.

"Oh, Josie, come see your stud coming over the hill!"

We ran out of camp as that lathered horse flesh made a complete charge around camp. Alex got out his rope, and I interfered with, "Alex, don't try to dally that horse down. He will go off like a gun. Let me try to gentle him some, and I'll get that saddle off." I went to my wagon, put my buckskins on, took my bonnet off, and let my hair fly. Alex gave me a small rope, and I intercepted my steed in mid-round.

Now isn't this something? A one hundred-pound woman trying to catch a grown stud. I got the feed bucket out and walked out on the prairie and stood quiet. That walleyed mess of sweat-lathered Owl Dung charged like I wasn't even there. Came to a sliding stop not ten feet in front of me, trembling. I crooned, took the bridle out of his sore mouth, looped my rope over his neck, and let the saddle drop in the grass. It was as if a completely different horse came out from under all that tack. I watered, watched as he rolled in the grass, and turned him loose. I thought he would never trust another robber in his life.

"Alex, find us a creek. I need to give my horse a good bath." The excitement was over, but the telling lasted for days (the day Momma caught a wild horse!).

Owl Dung and I had a good splashing bath in the next river, and I found where he had been beaten with a black snake, been scratched on his head from that Spanish bit. As long as I was around, he was fine, but don't mess with my horse.

Getting On

I come down off my cloud, and we got on with the drive. We had been on the trail seven days. The doctor thought we were making about eight miles a day. Fifty miles and we had lived a lifetime already. Nella and I traveled together most of the time so we could talk, but when we ran out of something to talk about, we just rode along silently enjoying the outing. East Kansas was famous for spring showers, and the weather didn't disappoint us. We looked forward to getting soaked to the skin and then being sun-dried like the trees. Doc would ride alongside and keep us awake with his droll conversations of some operation that he had preformed. His observations were at least revealing. That fine day Doc asked Nella if she was having morning sickness yet. Nella blanched and said she could choke them down so far. Here I was with Nella most of the time and never noticed what was going on. My morning sickness started in less than a week, and I had sympathy pains with her. Both of us could retch all morning just being around each other. The menfolk separated us, which helped, but I kept the same symptoms. Doc came around and looked at my eyes and ears and pronounced me with child too.

I don't have time for another boy! I thought.

Two expectant mothers on the trail, eight span of mules, two wagons, four boys on the ground, two husbands, one doctor, a milk cow and several cows with calf, my stud horse, and we could see the Plains Indians watching us watching them. I put on my too-tight buckskins and met them on a high plateau to talk the day along. My experience with The Hawk had gone before me to all the Plains Indians and they wanted to meet the woman that had Owl Dung. I let him have his head, and he cantered around some till I let him know that I was still boss. The Plains Indians wanted to trade him for several horses, but I told them he was a one-woman horse, which they didn't believe. I released Owl Dung and told him to stay close by; all the chiefs snickered and did the same thing. Owl Dung promptly corralled the loose stock and made for parts unknown. All the Indians thought, *Well, we walk.* I didn't want to trade any stock, and we broke up all walking toward the camps. I whistled my shrill best, and there came my stud in full gallop; the chiefs all looked on with open mouths at the trick we had pulled on them. I relented and rounded up their loose mounts, and we parted company with good feelings.

We had a disturbance that night with a loose horse running through our camp. I put the feeling aside until daylight showed us a young field-dressed deer that the Plains brothers had sent us.

We won't starve in eastern Kansas, I thought.

Nella and I were as pregnant as two trail mothers could be. We got back together riding in the same wagon; the talk shifted to baby things. We left the menfolk out of that talk with a lot of giggles being snickered.

Alex came in that evening with the news that Owl Dung was missing again! We hadn't seen any more Indians and I knew he wouldn't stand for another person riding him. We had to keep moving, and I thought, *Well, I've lost him for good.*

That sorry horse flesh came back during the night, whimpering around like some sick mule. I still didn't think too much about him till daylight showed us that stud had been horsing around. He had been in a fight with another stud and smelled to high heaven! We got on the trail, and the thought hit me that I didn't need a stud. I needed a gentlin' done on my stud! Doc came by in one of his talking moods.

Now is the time for some help! I thought.

"Doc, I need—"

"Josie, I'm not going to help you with your stud. If you want to cut him that is your business."

How does he always know what I'm going to say before I say it? I shrugged and he spoke up, "Oh, okay, but this is last time I help you neuter a male animal."

We stopped early that day, got a hold of Owl Dung, and fed him some sweet feed with my secret Sang. We soon had a snoring stud laid out on the prairie. I first got out a heavy halter and tied him to the back axle. Doc and I neutered that stud right there in the grass. All the boys watched with wide eyes at what their mother and Doc were doing. . Nella lost her dinner over on the other side of the wagons. Doc and I wanted to find another name beside Owl Dung. We finally came up with Bob. We had bobbed us a horse on the way to my own home.

We had us a sore horse the next morning; in fact, he looked like he didn't know which end hurt the most. The halter had a good workout; Bob calmed down by midmorning and followed the back wagon peacefully. We didn't make too much ground that day, but we kept on the trail south. The Stranger Creek led us right to the flooded Kansas River, which was muddy, tree choked, and had lots of cattle floating right down the center. We backtracked up to the clean Stranger and decided to ride out the storm while washing our clothes. I got the menfolk to help me start a smudge fire and make jerky of the young deer.

Nella had all the kids help her wash clothes in the creek. I tended Old Bob, as we called him by now, and he gentled right down into a good, dependable horse. I asked Alex when we got on the trail again for some light harness; I wanted to train my Old Bob to pull a surrey.

"Josie, that Indian pony is wild, and nobody can tame a wild horse."

"Yes, Alex, you are right, but you will see, he will do it for me." An all-knowing nod was all I got from my husband that day as he muttered under his breath.

"Yes, I suppose he will for you."

We stayed on the creek banks until the Kansas River slowed down to a drawl. We really liked the stay over, as we needed to rest up. I lost track of the days and decided not to date but just write in my journal.

As summer made us all hot, Nella and I became so swollen that we decided the walking would do us both good. This slowed down progress, but we had to have some relief. One of the long days the men folk decided we needed to show more guns on the trail. They took the boys along during the day and showed them how to handle Long Tom shotguns. They even put the boys into the back wagon to practice how to load and shoot the Flint Lock black powder guns.

We had guns going off in the middle of the day, and one day they even hit a big rabbit.

"We eat rabbit!" the camp rang. Yep, Mr. Jack Rabbit made stew of the day. Nella made rabbit dressing and rabbit gravy. We found poke greens and a few blackberries that I smashed down with sugar. The boys thought they had fed the wagon train that day. Yes, we ate like kings, but the biggest thought was they were learning to guard the wagons.

Eight months and sixteen days flowed by until Nella and I delivered within a week of each other. I named my boy Leo, and Nella picked out Nelliene for her girl, the very first girl for Slim and Nella. The birthin' slowed us down, and we didn't make near that eight miles a day we set out to. The menfolk started to look for a "winter over" spot for the two families; we found several creeks that seemed to have plenty of flow. Sugar Creek fit us, as the men unloaded a sod cutter and made us a sod house to keep the snow from freezing us. A corral was erected for the stock at night, and Alex stocked up on sweet feed to keep them coming in each morning.

A trading post supplied our "winter over" needs, and we hunkered down as the first snow storms kept us inside. The boys were eager to shoot their guns, and we had deer, rabbits, squirrels, a stinky antelope, a cow buffalo, of which I scraped the hide, tanned, and made us a large robe. Nella and I nursed our babies into chunky kids. Doc got into his element and nursed us all to the peak of health. Our stock got so ornery during the snow that Alex let them out to slide on the ice-covered hills. They came back in that night so sore they could hardly walk.

Sam had several fishing contests in Sugar Creek that winter. We had always been told you can't catch a catfish when it is cold. Foot, we had so much fried catfish that we got to believing that we could swim faster. Nella got to freezing catfish on the roof of our sod house, worked well till a mink got his share of our fish. This led to catching mink and selling hides at the trading post. A trapline was set, and we caught coyotes, badgers, a dark little animal they called a fisher, and plenty of rabbits were shot by the boys' .22 rifle.

Christmas caught us all by surprise, as we had lost track of the time; days and months just didn't seem to matter. We celebrated by reading Luke the second chapter and hugging each other, and the boys memorized the Bible version of the Christ Child. The menfolk ran out of tobacco. We were running out of staples when it was decided we would take a wagon into the trading post and restock. Doc, Slim, and the boys wanted to stay at home and hone their shooting skills. Alex, Nella, and I had made a long list. We had measured all the boys and bought good, heavy boots for the next leg of the trail. Alex said we were going to get into flint hill country, and we didn't need sore feet from the rocks.

Slim and Alex set up the forge and shoed all the walking stock. Alex was always so patient with his mules. They used all the shoes they had and had to go back to the trading post for more. The old trader at the post got to asking Alex who was doing the shoeing. Slim and Alex admitted that they had brought the trade from Braymer, Missouri. Not to miss any opportunity for business, the old trader asked the men if they could shoe his teams. A deal was struck that day to get into the business of shoeing horses; little did I know that Doc and I would get busy too. Our kids came down with the whooping cough, which soon spread to our complete wagon train. Doc and I knew we better get started soon on a remedy, he made some cough syrup that didn't do a thing. I started to run a high fever and was in bed full time with dreams of times past, and I wound up dreaming about my time with Raven. I couldn't get the idea out of my hot head, I told Doc to get into my herb chest and look for some black straws; his first reactions when he opened my chest was one of disgust and disbelieve.

"What's this Indian got me into now?" He came back holding that small shock of grass. "Josie, don't tell me you are going to start eating grass?"

I was so lightheaded I finally mumbled, "Doc, don't argue with me! Break some of the black straws into a cup, fill with hot water, let steep until the water is good and dark. Now, Doc, no matter what I say or do, you get that whole cup down me!"

"Josie, I'm not going to feed you anything that's not proven."

"*Doc!*"

He fed me the worst-tasting swill until I almost gave the whole cupful back. I was worn out from the excitement and fell into a deep stupor. I lost the rest of the day and woke up the next morning cool but weak as a kitten. My throat felt like raw beef, and I was sure my teeth had hair growing on them! The rest of the clan was coughing their heads off. I suggested Doc find some moonshine to add to his cough syrup so the bunch could get some rest. Slim took Doc back to the trading post and brought back a gallon of the clear whisky, minus some for Slim. A quick mixture with his homemade syrup put snores in the air. I got my cupful and dreamed the most relaxed time I had ever had. Slim got back into the gallon jug, and I had to hide the rest for future use. We moped around for a day of two then found out the whole trading post needed Doc and me to come help with the epidemic. I took my black straws but never needed them. We nursed and doctored the post back to health. A nice couple lost a baby to the whooping cough of '91, but we did the best we could as greening time came upon us. Alex shoed enough horses to trade for new lever-action guns, all the same caliber. We got on the trail again in the spring of '91.

Leo and Nelliene came through the winter doing what babies do, getting fat and sassy. It's always a thrill when they start talking their baby talk. I guess you could say Nella and I schooled both families while on the trail to Oklahoma. I don't know how much good we did, but the boys and one girl complained about having to have lessons on the trail. Doc was the best storyteller, and he mixed his stories with so much medical jargon that they never suspected he was telling about some operation.

FLINT HILLS

Our entrance into the flint hills of eastern Kansas came overnight. The rolling hills were so pretty with the spring flowers, and there seemed to be springs coming out of each new hill. We saw ragtag clumps of Indians trying to find buffalo, and I felt so sorry for the Indians. My heart bled, but we kept to ourselves and they only paused to glance at us. I was always on the lookout for herbs. The windy Kansas flint hills would only produce wild onions and that ever-present turkey grass by the field full. I dried plenty of onions to plant in Oklahoma. The boys kept practicing with their new rifles; a good rabbit could be stewed with the onions for a tasty meal. The clear creeks we crossed produced the best goggle-eyed perch. Nella would fry a handful of bacon strips with the fish, as I got to making fry bread by the basketful. Our Jerz, had freshened up that spring, and we had all the milk we could drink. Much to the delight of Leo, and Nelliene, they filled up to the brim at each feeding.

The boots that we had bought at the trading post sure saved the day. After the first week walking in those rocks, I thought to myself, *I hope the boots last until we get to my own home!* My Old Bob had gotten his first pair of shoes last winter and sure paraded around with me out on the prairie. I had been leaving the buggy harness on him. It took all I could do, but he finally settled down. I cut a small tree one day and let him drag that. I didn't know his eyes could get so big!

I really think all we did was stare at the prairie dogs. We had to trail along the creeks and rivers to keep out of the prairie dog towns. We would travel all of one day in one town. I remembered that Raven told me not to eat a prairie dog for fear of getting the plague.

The first smells of human waste started coming with the southeast winds. Doc and I worried about the plagues we had read about the only thing we knew to do was to keep on a southern tack. We saw several wagon trains going east. One evening we made camp around a big spring. It wasn't long before the wagons made a complete circle. We feasted on gossip that evening. You could hear anything! It seemed that the smell that was in the air was Kansas City, Kansas, sitting across the Kansas River. We all shuttered at the thought.

A woman was trying to deliver a child, and it took Doc and me to come to the conclusion that the woman was too small. Doc got out his instruments and gave the woman a stick to chew on and started right in cutting through the skin. The menfolk helped hold her down, and a small girl-child was stillborn that night. By the next morning we had a double burial with the woman holding the child on her bosom. The shallow grave in the rocks was dug along the side of the trail, packed down, and all the wagons ran over the site. I dared not ask why till I got Alex alone, and he explained they wanted the gravesite hidden from the animals for all times. I kept those words to myself and reasoned trail customs were so cruel sometimes.

We traveled in silence until the smell freshened with a southwest wind. The wind screeched around our wagons so much that we thought we would lose our hearing. About an hour before dark the wind died to absolute silence. Man and beast were so glad for the relief as we turned in early and slept an exhausted sleep.

We traveled all the next day and found a clean creek with lots of Indian sign along the banks. Just as we made camp, a troop of Pottawatomie paced in the creek for water. I hurriedly took my hair down, got out the buckskins, and was an Indian again. I surprised them by signing for a palaver. Their reservation was southwest, another day's ride. I invited them to eat and stay the night. They didn't have anything but two prairie chickens, which we added to the pot of stew. Nella made cornpone cakes, we milked Jerz, and in no time we fed our guests. We tried to talk to each other but wound up signing in the firelight. Doc sewed up one of the brave's leg and bound it with an old shirt tail. The braves asked about Old Bob, and I called him to me for their inspection. It was about then they remembered the tale about The Hawk giving his prize stud to a woman. They really wanted to rub Old Bob, but he was not going to have anything to do with those strange smells.

I heard the troop leave early the next morning. Alex started to get out from under the wagon when I whispered, "He'll be back in no time." Daylight came with us trying to get the coffee perking when I heard my Old Bob coming in at a full gallop with a nice Indian bridle still on his head! I kept the prize, with its eagle feathers on one side, to remember the braves.

Oh well, I thought, *they will make it back to the reservation for their next meal. You reckon they will tell about losing a prize horse?*

We made good time along Lightning Creek and saw several bands of Cherokee, Neosho, and Osage. They never bothered us, and we kept to ourselves. The boys kept practicing with the rifles, and not much was missed by them. They even had a porcupine cornered one day Alex happened by, and none of them got stuck. We saw the commotion, and I asked what the matter was.

"Oh, Momma, come quick! We have something with stickers all over it!"

Nella and I got there just in time to see one of the boys shoot a porcupine. I got all the menfolk back and told them to leave well enough alone till old Mr. Sticker was completely dead. Nella and I took over and plucked every quill from that hide, skinned the carcass, and started boiling the best pork-tasting soup. All the boys, two men, one woman, and one girl turned up their nose and squalled, "We's not chewing on that thang." I very politely said, "Okay, that's fine with me, because I was going to eat pig come suppertime."

Quiet, turned-up noses, till the pork flavoring scented the air. One by one the hungries came by the big iron pot and surmised that it was being cooked for supper. I took all the kids and we made a game of finding wild garlic, onions, water lily bulbs, sun roots, skunk cabbage, and some tender shoots from a berry bush. Nella and Nelliene found strawberries growing around the limestone outcrops. All in all our supper came from the land, and we had left plenty to grow on. My porcupine soup with all the trimmings fed us that night, and we all went to bed under the wagons with swollen paunches.

Buffalo

We heard and felt the thundering herd in the night as we tried to sleep. We had camped on the east side of the Lightning Creek, and we felt the buffalo on the west side they were so close. As daybreak came we saw how close they were; those massive heads with bodies to match made us uncomfortable to be so exposed. We needn't have worried, for the creek was deep and sharp-sided; we were in no danger. I had one buffalo robe we used for a ground cover and could have used another. Alex and Slim looked the situation over and decided to pass on the herd. There was so many and close to our wagons. I thought we were passing up a good opportunity, but we had to think about our families. We traveled all that day and part of the next before we started to see the big birds in the sky. I couldn't think what had happened to gather that many vultures. I whistle-stopped Old Bob and Alex, and I cantered downwind of the birds. The southwest wind told us not to go any farther; the smell of rotting flesh was going to be a lot worse than we wanted. We backtracked to get upwind and were not prepared for the sight of a buffalo herd that had been slaughtered for its tongue and tail. We saw so many scavengers on the carcasses we couldn't count them all. I lost my want for another buffalo from the mess on the prairie.

Our silent retreat caught us up with our party, and we trudged on. Supper that night brought more questions than answers. The only thing we could think was there were a bunch of buffalo skinners out for the hides, and they decided to take the tongues instead. I could only think of the Indians that one hundred head of buffalo would feed, clothe, and sustain for months on end. We pressed on the next day and found a crippled cow buffalo on the trail. The boys got out their new rifles, and I soon had my new robe packed in salt and ready to be cleaned the next day. We dined on the back strap, all we could stand, and filled the big pot and I cooked that all night for meat the next day. We set up camp alongside the creek and staked out the hide to dry. We had forgotten what day it was, but we set the day aside to have early mass and refresh our clothes while we all took our turns scrapping the buffalo hide. I found a walnut tree in the creek bottom and had the boys gather all the hulls we could get into a washtub. Boiling hot water, walnut hulls, oak leaves, and a green buffalo hide tanned us a very dark, cured buffalo hide.

We heard the guns going off the next day and got on the trail as soon as we could pack up. We knew to get away from another buffalo slaughter as soon as we could. The skinners were going to kill the whole herd, and we weren't going to have anything to do with it.

I felt for the Indian tribes that would starve the next winter and couldn't do anything to help.

Indiana Territory

As we crossed into Indian Territory just outside the Chetopa Trading Post, I asked what the land was like farther into the territory. Depended who you talked to, the stories were running so rampant. One that we really liked was the unassigned Indian land of the Pawnees was to open for settlement along the Cimarron River September 16, 1893. I slept a very light sleep that night by willing my mind to center on to my own home. We quickened our step to make the spring getting ready to claim our land along the Cimarron River. The land was changing from open prairie to oak woods that shut out the sunlight again. Our southwest tack took us over the Verdigris, Caney, and Bird, and we never wanted for water.

We saw countless Indians; we didn't pay them attention, nor them us. They all seemed so threadbare. Traveling was too easy, I considered. We had been told not to trust any Indians. Alex and Slim talked about putting out scouts to travel during the day, a night rider during the night. Nobody thought they could stay up all night. I answered that problem.

"I'll tell Old Bob to feed around the camp at night and to warn us if there is any problem."

"Yeah right, Josie. You just go ahead, talk to your horse!"

I did! Talked to him in Sac and Fox, Cherokee, made up a few signs, and sent him on his way. All I got from the menfolk were shaking heads.

Wasn't too many more stops till Old Bob kept perking his ears, never said much, and I knew that this was the night. I told Alex, as he did admit that the hair was standing up on his neck; he bedded the boys around in the trees and covered them up with brush. He gave each one a Long Tom flint rifle loaded with powder only. Their saddle guns were at ready in case they were needed. I got out a few pots and pans and strung them out in the trees just in case.

We settled down early under the wagons and had a good nap until Old Bob blew his hot breath down my neck. The Indian side of me came awake in a heartbeat. Alex was awake when the first pan hit the other. The moon was close to dark, and one of the tied-up pans swung down off a limb and rang like a bell with someone's head as the clapper. Of all the swearing coming from that quarter, it was not an Indian's voice; it was a white man's! The boys let loose the first volley. We couldn't see a thing because of all the smoke, and then those repeater rifles spoke with a sharper crack up in the air. We could hear their retreat, then Old Bob got into the act with his kicking, bucking, and stomping. We heard several cries out in the woods, then complete silence settled in as Old Bob came back. We lit a lantern to check on the boys. There was the lot smiling; they had won a battle. We looked each over and not a scratch. Old Bob had blood on his muzzle where he must have bit somebody. All the mules had come in at daylight for their morning ration like nothing happened.

Alex tried to settle everybody down, but the tall tales were being spread around like rain. Doc came walking in from his tree house, kind of sheepishly; must have slept till the old Long Tom's woke up the countryside. Daylight told the rest of the story. The guy who had been hit with my frying pan was still out lying in the brush. We tried to wake him, but the smell of rot gut whisky ran us off. Slim took the guy's boots off and burnt them, took brush and covered that drunken sot completely up, and we had breakfast and left him so his buddies had something to look for.

Our run-in with the lawless was a good wakeup call for the coming days. Even the boys got to watching for the buggers standing behind the clumps of oak scrub trees. The boys and their sharpshooting supplied us with game from off the land. We saw more and more Indians in the distance. Never were we bothered or even close. We realized all those old wife's tales were just that, tales. We crossed the Arkansas River close to the Cleveland Trading Post and decided to "winter over" for an early start in the spring of '93.

The menfolk cut logs, and we built a log home in Indian Territory on the south side of the river. Slim and Alex let it be known that they were setting a blacksmith shop up to shoe horses and fix wagons. Seemed that was just what the travelers needed. I couldn't count the horses that were shod, wagons repaired, kids that were born, and colds that ran their courses among the wagon trains. We fished out of the Arkansas River and got ready for the run into Indian Territory.

We had a very mild winter. I kept the boys busy picking up pecans, walnuts, and hickory nuts and selling them to the trading post. This kept both families well-supplied with traded goods. Come green-up time in late March, we got the traveling urge again. We said "stay well" to all the friends we had made just in time for the spring flood on the Arkansas. We were glad to be across that old muddy thing. We had seen creeks at flood stage before, but this was lots worse. The boys and girl started in counting the dead animals that day and got to over a hundred. This did not count the tree stumps and all, log houses, rail fences, and a few wooden wagons. We got on the trail to get away from the flood and took an almost southern route into the first settlement of Teriton. We bought some staples, and Alex bought a whole keg of horseshoes. I could see he was going to keep busy the upcoming spring and summer down on the Cimarron River.

As we came into view of Silver City, we camped out under the cottonwood trees and about spent the rest of the spring there. That old itchy feeling came up on both Alex and me, and we knew we best be looking around. The settlement was alive with settlers going on west into Indian Territory. I got my mount with me wearing my buckskins and headband. Alex, Slim, and I set out to explore the land. Traveling light, we made good time into the Creek Nation and heard that old dragon off in the distance. We finally surmised it was a steam whistle for heavy equipment. We had heard the same whistle on the Missouri and Mississippi paddleboats. It had to be checked out as we rode down an old haul road, we knew we were on the right track. All the same equipment that came to our farm to cut logs in Missouri was scattered out along the road. That old dragon squealed again as we walked our horses into view of the sawmill. The mules didn't seem to pay much attention, but my Old Bob pitched a fit until I crooned my "behave" sound to him. The operator shut the sawmill down for the day and came to meet us with a stretched-out hand.

"Why, howdy! You'll come set a spell and water your stock."

We introduced all around and found out Ole and his wife, Sara, lived right there by the sawmill.

Ole discovered that I was an Indian; he took off his hat and apologized there in the middle of the road.

"I'm a sorry dog to scare your horse. Wow, lookie what we have here. A real spotted Indian horse. *Sara!* Come lookie at what's come walkin' onto our place."

You could have blown me over with a feather as this real nice Indian woman came out of their house. Sara didn't even look at us; she walked up to Old Bob and started rubbing him down with her apron. Old Bob liked a good quick rub, and Sara rubbed him down, even his back legs. Sara turned on me and demanded to know how I got Owl Dung from The Hawk.

Ole could see that a complete explanation had to be made and invited all to sit under his shade trees. I told the complete story of finding the old man out on the prairie, the loose horse, and riding Owl Dung into the Indian camp of The Hawk.

Sara stopped me and said, "You mean you rode this spotted horse right into the camp?" Sara stammered her next words. "Josie, this is an unbelievable story. That horse is a man killer, he will stomp on anyone that tries to get close to him. Now, Josie, I want to ride your horse."

I tried to stop her as she swung on barebacked. Old Bob bunched up until Sara crooned and all was well. She didn't even lift the rope; she just moved her knees and Old Bob remembered her!

I hope Sara never comes to my house. She could steal Old Bob, I thought to myself. Sara loped him and let him get a drink, and then she came back and took off the Indian bridle and shooed him back into the spring. A quick whistle from Sara, and Old Bob was back under the shade trees.

"I see Owl Dung hasn't forgotten his early training," Sara mused. What you call him now that he is a gelding?"

Taken aback, I merely said, "Old Bob."

"Old Bob, Old Bob, yes, that's a good name. You have had him bobbed."

"No," I said. "I bobbed him myself."

Sara took her turn to look blanched. "You? Why, it would take a healer to do that."

"Okay," I retorted.

Ole took over after that exchange and exclaimed, "Ladies, ladies, let's have something cool to drink, and we'll get caught up with some talkin'."

Sara and I got over being bashful so quick there wasn't time to really get acquainted. She invited me into the house. We got some of that cool spring water that ran through her house, and we exchanged talk just like the menfolk were doing. We explained why we were here and that we needed to be looking around.

"What are you looking for?" Ole asked. As we told our story, he kept saying, "Yes ... yes ... okay ... well, I'll be."

We ran down and he started in with the telling that yes, there was land to had over on the west side of the Cimarron River in the land run of '93 just a few months from now.

"Tell you what, spend the night right here and get an early start in the morning and you can be into Indian Territory in a couple of hours after daybreak. Have a good look around on the west side of the Cimarron River for several miles both north and south. If I remember right, there are several good springs about a mile or two away from the river. If I was you, I would have a sharp eye out for the militia. They are to run all the Sooners out of Indian Territory before the run," Ole said.

We exclaimed that we knew all there was to know about the militia and how they were bent on running all the Indians out of Missouri. As Ole went on, he said, "You will find the opposite of that here. They want all the Indians to stay in Oklahoma. In fact, if you see the militia, let them see Josie and they will leave her alone."

Alex took Ole up on his offer and said that if Ole had anything to fix, he would be back to help him out.

We tried to get out the next morning before daylight. Sara already had a good breakfast and a sack of food for the next two days. I tried to pay her for it, but she said to come back and we'd settle up.

Our trip by Oilton, then on to the Cimarron River, came by in due time. We crossed that muddy river to huge stands of oak trees. We rode abreast and made the complete inspection before midday. We saw several good springs, but I was looking for one back in the oak stands. As we were moving out, we caught a glimpse of the militia over on yon hill. I looked my most stern look and ambled out into the open, like bait, and here they came at speed till they saw me. I moved out in the open away from my Alex and Slim so they could get around me. They circled some and tried to talk to me. I acted dumb and signed for them to leave me alone.

The sergeant in charge looked Old Bob over and talked to his platoon. "Look there, boys. These Indians have better horses then we do."

Old Bob was okay so far, but when I kneed him a little, he looked that sergeant over as though he were saying, "I'll take a bite out of your leg if you bother us."

The sergeant moved back and said, "Boys, let's get out of here. There's nothing we should do to this Indian." They showed me their backsides, much to the relief of Alex and Slim.

Pawnee Trail

Our venture into the land brought us to the halfway point between Pawnee and Sapulpa, called the Pawnee Trail. A large spring in the hillside furnished water for the travelers as they traveled the oak woods by the Cimarron River. Old campfires long since burnt out dotted the camp area, and several clearings were ready for overnight stays. We shied away from such a public place and dry camped back in the woods. We heard the militia camping off in the distance; they were the only ones that made that much noise. We talked most of the night and decided we would try to make the run for 160 acres around the big spring. As we were leaving the next morning, a big wagon train with lumber was seen heading for Sapulpa. The militia cornered them on the west side of the Cimarron and told them to keep out until the run in September. The wagon master got huffy and tried to tell the sergeant that they had traveled the same trail for thirty years hauling lumber and they weren't about the stop now.

Mr. Sergeant got right back into his face and ordered the man arrested; he took him on the east side of the Cimarron River and said, "Don't come back this way."

As the wagon train got to the river crossing, Mr. Huffy had cooled off and told his help not to worry, for he would take care of the militia. They trudged on toward Sapulpa out of our sight, and I thought right then, *I bet this fracas is not over.*

We heard later that a wagon master had been thrown in the brig for disobeying orders. That would have put him in jail long enough for the run to be over and maybe he would get out of Oklahoma.

As we were standing still, Slim spied a big patch of cattails and made the mention that they only grew where there was a constant supply of water. We cantered into the middle of the patch and ran into a deep spring. Alex and I knew this was the place for us! We made the den of the dragon before dark and spent the night with Ole and Sara. Ole was ready for Alex with a pocket full of questions.

"Where did you go? What did you see? What do you think? Alex, let me see your hands." Ole rubbed his hairy jaw. "Just like I figured out, you boys are blacksmiths!"

"Yes," said Alex. "We are looking for a place to set up business on the west side of the river."

"Hmm," said Ole. "What are you going to do between now and the run over into Payne County?"

Alex explained that we were leaving plenty of time to look over the land that was offered and would try to work something out.

Ole smiled his best and started in with, "Boys, I have an idea that could be useful to all the families. You boys go get the rest of your family, move into our shade tree park, set up your forge, tables, and anvils, whatever you need to be in business. I guarantee you more work than you can do in a lifetime of blacksmithing, and I will be your best customer."

Alex, Slim, and I talked the offer over and made a decision to do just as Ole suggested. Slim spoke up and said that he would help Alex set up his blacksmith shop and then he wanted to get on to Guthrie to see if he could get some land there. We all nodded our approval.

We asked Ole if he would lead the Sunday mass each Sunday morning. Ole looked over the spring and told us that he wasn't a priest or preacher, but he would lead the singing and pray when called upon. We sealed the deal by hugging each other all the way around.

Daylight Mass

We had daylight mass the next morning, and could that Ole lead out in his deep baritone voice. I had never been to an evangelical service before, but the time set aside to worship the Lord that morning was well-spent. Our riding stocks were well-rested as we threaded our way back the way we had come. A short day's ride put us into the arms of the boys camped out by Silver City. They were so glad to see us so soon; we had told them we would be gone maybe two weeks. We slam-banged all our camp gear in the wagons and made for the campsite of the sawmill dragon.

The oak trees slowed us down, and we camped where we could hear the dragon scream. I'm not one to lie, tell gossip, cheat, or bargain with the devil, but it was too good to pass up. Alex started talking about the dragon that was down in the woods somewhere. Slim told about hearing him scream for miles around. I wondered out loud what a dragon would look like. The boys, Nella, Doc, and Nelliene all started in looking behind each tree! Quitting time scream set this bunch on edge! Nelliene ran to her mother, the boys all gathered around their dads, Doc squinted his eyes; I had to look the other way! Slim took over and said, "Well, that's it for today that ole dragon won't scream again until morning."

We ate what we had while the boys built a fire that would keep the dragons away till daylight. Nella, Doc, and I were up to fix a good breakfast at daylight. Fresh milk, cornmeal mush, finished up with sourdough toast and jelly got the kids ready for the first scream of the day. As the dragon screamed, our boys and girl started milling around each other, our stock never missed a step, and the grownups were having the laugh of the day. The horses, mules, and cows never missed a step. The boys were all walking along. They jumped, milled around, ran into each other. All the grownups were laughing their heads off as that scream came from just around the bend. Doc and Nella had figured out the dragon as Ole came out to greet the company. Sara's donkey had let them know when we broke camp and had made several runs around his pen. Sara and Ole came out and hugged each one of the kids, us, my horse, but they stayed away from Alex's old heehaw mules. Everyone talked at once as we set up a more permanent camp. We figured to stay three or four months to ready ourselves for the run into Indian Territory September 16, 1893.

Sara, Nella, and I started cooking in the bunkhouse together where the cast iron wood cookstove sat, with an oven. I had missed my cookstove while on the trail and made the best of my time catching up. I can't remember what I cooked first but always cooked in large quantities. There were three men, three women, seven boys, one girl, and one horse that ate whatever was left. Old Bob was always ready for a handout; his favorite was syrup on anything. Alex turned his mules in with their donkey, and they were ready to set up shop. Alex and Slim got their blacksmith shop set up under the park oak trees; they even ran water through one corner into a big barrel then out to a creek. Ole had plenty of coal for the forge. The boys got used to the dragon scream-ing each morning and evening. We all stood around the mill the first few days with our mouths wide open, watching the sights. The mill hands had dinner with us on the picnic benches, and life got into the next phase of getting ready for the run.

True to Slim's word, the blacksmith shop was up and running before him and Nella started their trek to Guthrie. Sara treated all of us alike coming or going—everybody got an Indian hug. She called everybody around when they were ready to travel, fed them one last time, and sent a picnic lunch for later in the day.

"Everybody gather round. Let's have a word of prayer for the journey of Slim and Nella and the chil-dren," she would say. Sara always sent them on with the same prayer, *For God so loved the world that he gave his only begotten son that whosoever believed would have everlasting life. Amen.*

Ole had to clear his voice and sang:

Bless be the tide that binds,
our hearts in Christen love.
The fellowship of kindred
minds are like to that above.

Slim and Nella had become such good friends, we hated the day they left just in front of the dust. I carried that lump in my throat, and Sara and I didn't tell one tale the whole day. The next morning we fixed sour-dough pancakes, fresh maple syrup, warm milk, and butter we had been making from old Jerz. Sara clapped her hands and said, "That's it! We mope no more. This is the day that the Lord has made, let us be glad and rejoice in it."

"I want you boys to go up on the hillside and pick us a good pail of strawberries. Josephine, dress them boys in long pants, long-sleeved shirts, and boots. There are enough chiggers up in those hills to last a year. Ole, I want you to dab coal oil on all their cuffs, waistline, and hats. Give them a jug of spring water to last all morning. Now, boys, your mother and I have got a lifetime of talking to catch up on this morning. You can come back when you have got your pail full, but don't bother us until we call dinner. Alex and Doc, I fear for your health. Ole has got so much for you to do. Why don't you'll make plans to get started repairing whatever is broken or wore out? Now you'll remember I don't give out orders very often, but today is Josie and Sara's day!"

All the menfolk scattered like quail afraid she would think of something else to do. Sara very sweetly spoke to me, "Josie, we got the menfolk out of our hair. Let's have another cup of coffee and we'll start right in talking."

This is my kind of lady.

LIFE'S STORIES

We shared life stories that took us all the way back to us starting to remembering. How similar the Indians stories seemed to be. Just change the names and I could have fit right into Sara's. She cried when I showed her the faded scars on my face of years past and told her how Doc had lovingly smoothed them out and saved me from embarrassment. Sara asked me how old Doc was; so help me I didn't know. We compared thoughts and figured he was close to seventy years old but never complained one whimper.

"Josie, you know he's going to die soon?"

"No! No! He can't. I still owe him so much."

"No, no, Josie, he has been paid in full. Watch the way he smiles when he sees your boys. Those boys are the children he could never have, and he loves them as his own."

"Sara, I wonder why he never married."

"Josie, let me tell you the way of his tribe. He was

set aside at birth to be sent off for an education to help his tribe. During the Indian repression he lost his family. You and Alex are his family now. Just accept the fact and let's use his talent while we can."

The boys had started coming in hot and tired with a pail full of ripe berries.

"Boys, go get the menfolk. All of you take a spring bath, wash real good with lye soap, and we'll bring you clean clothes and blankets. Let's pretend you are a spoiled tribe wanting something to eat."

All of the menfolk got into the act of taking baths with the kids; this took the dirt and chiggers off. Clean clothes all the way around felt much better, and that started the howling for something to eat. Sara fixed fry bread and beans; for dessert I smashed the strawberries with plenty of sugar and then poured thick cream on each bowlful. We all sat around the bunkhouse table after dinner; then our whole clan got out the pallets and fell over in the floor with naps all the way around. Needless to say, we needed the rest; I praised the Lord for Sara and her different ways.

We sat by a fire that night and roasted some kind of meat that sure smelled like pork, but I didn't ask any questions. Alex asked the blessing for the night, and I ran my beads while saying the evening prayers. Sleep among the oak trees brought dreams of moving to my own home that night, and I could finally get a dream picture of where my home would be.

Alex and Ole fixed everything on the mill. There was never any money passed hands, but the trading started each morning during first coffee. Sara and I enjoyed the banter and knew both families would be blessed. Alex had unloaded the farm wagon and filled it with lumber of all kinds and sizes. He filled one sack with iron works; I didn't ask or interfere with his black-smithing or carpenter skills. I knew it would take us all to build a new homestead. There was one thing that puzzled me: Alex built a waterproof chest, fastened it to the bottom of the farm wagon, stacked cut lumber all over it, and you would never know it was there. I asked one day, "Alex, what is that chest in the center of the wagon?"

He shrugged and said, "That is part of our new home."

I believed him and went on with the meals.

The boys went out every day with their new guns and kept us well-supplied with meat; we would find a young field-dressed deer or porcupine hanging in the park. Sara would smile just so and state, "Hmm, won-der what those bucks want?" I awoke one morning early and started the cookstove heating to make coffee when a horse stomped out in the park. I looked out; there were several bucks lined up waiting on Sara to come out. I untied my hair, stepped out, and signed to have some coffee. I noticed a small girl lying across the rump of the lead pony. Sara had stirred by then, and we took that limp girl down. Only then did we notice the child inside her. We did a quick check and found out the girl was in labor but much too small to deliver. All the bucks had slid down by then and sat on the half-log benches, never saying a word. I served them sweet cof-fee and they left as quietly as they came.

Doc stirred out from under the wagon, and we let him in on the secret. Doc looked on and quietly got his bag out of the wagon. Sara stepped in front of him and said, "Doc, you know that girl is too small to have that child. What are you going to do?"

I could see Doc swell to his full height of five foot

two inches and proclaim that he and Josie were going to save both the mother's and child's lives. I remembered the last time he had cut a child out of the womb and we lost both lives. Sara gave us free reign to do as we thought right. Doc washed his hands and told me that the mother needed to be asleep to save their lives. I got my bag of herbs, made some sweet tea and the mother soon was fast asleep. By then Sara was all eyes and helped get the operation over with. A quick slice of the outside skin and the swollen womb came into sight. Sara said that was the first time she had seen the child bed while still in the mother. Doc soon had a squalling boy by the feet. We tied the cord, cleaned him up, and he was soon nursing his mother's milk. Doc stitched the womb and skin back together, washed his hands, and ordered some porcupine with four eggs and thick sourdough toast with strong coffee. Sara and I just stood there with our hands on our hips and shook our heads. If that old sawbones wanted breakfast, we guessed we could do that. By midmorning the mother was awake, hungry, and ready to go back to the Indian camp. Doc looked her over and said to Sara and I, "Tomorrow you take a buggy ride over the hill and take this young mother and child home. She shouldn't walk up that hill." Yes, Sara and I delivered the new mother to her husband. I was introduced to the chief of the clan, and we signed our good-byes. I didn't know then if that was good or bad, but my Indian Territory practice of midwife started with a new Indian baby boy that day.

Sara cornered me that same day and demanded to know where I had gotten the Sang. I confessed that we grew it in Missouri and asked if she wanted some.

"Hump! In a pig's eye I do!"

I got back in my herb chest with her hanging over my shoulder. I gave her a whole plant, seeds and all. You would have thought I had given her a gold coin, she smiled so.

"Josie, let me look in your chest, please!"

Do you suppose she knows all the plants? I thought. Sara took her time and named each one except the black straws that I had. I explained it was for black straw tea, used mainly to control fever. Sara put her hand over her mouth, exclaimed she had heard about it, but never had any or had even seen it. I didn't have much, but I looked in another drawstring bag and gave her a few seeds that she could plant. Holding the treasures to her bosom, she went to the bunkhouse where she stashed the herbs.

"Josie, we need to take a walk over the hill. I want to show you something." The boys took their guns, and we strolled through the woods into a glade of all the herbs that I used. We didn't have the same names, but they were used for the same cures. I got to the ginseng and said I didn't have any. She promptly took her pointed stick and gave me several roots. It was my turn to put them in my apron; we knew a good trade was made by all.

By then the boys had noticed a troop of Indians headed our way and gathered in front of us with guns at ready. We called them off and said they were friends and not to act bossy. Not a one of the braves were armed except with bows and arrows, which intrigued the boys, and we all sat in the grass and signed to each other. Sara asked about the papoose that was born the other night. One of the youngest braves turned that special red embarrassed look and signed that his Night Bird and Big Mouth were doing fine. Then he put Sara on the spot and asked, "What is the long red mark on Night Bird?"

Sara drew large circles in the sky, a small round one down lower, and signed that there was a great healer in our camp who had put his mark on the stomach of Night Bird so she could have Big Mouth. I again thought,

Oh, bulltail, That's a bunch of trash. Tell him what really happened! Just as quick Sara gave me that "keep quiet, let well enough alone" look with her shy smile. I signed, asking the brave if he had any more wives who needed the same mark. I got those flashing brown eyes, and he signed, No, she got along fine!

My boys were enjoying the palaver; we parted the Indian company and went back to our own world, each one laughing at the other.

Getting Ready for the Run

The heat slowed down the days as summer came on strong; we did everything we could outside close to the spring water. Alex had a progression of horses to shoe; Ole kept the mill hands busy with sawing logs like crazy. There seemed to be a constant stream of wagons coming and going on the haul road. The boys kept their hunting skills on edge, and we enjoyed game from the hills. We sat down in the shade one day and made permanent plans to move over close to the Creek Territory to be ready to make the run of '93.

The word came on the wagon trains that we would have to get our numbers to Stillwater, register the deed, and then move on the land. We didn't want to make any mistakes, so it was decided to make a dry run to the Stillwater Land Office and back to see if there were any problems. Alex and I rode our horses across the Cimarron River right at daylight one morning and found people hiding out on the land we wanted. The militia was everywhere, running them out of Indian Territory. I was riding Old Bob with my buckskins and headband. Alex hid in a patch of woods, and I rode the border of the quarter-section that we wanted. Of course the militia cornered me and tried to run me out. I played dumb; they soon realized I didn't understand English and left me alone. The same sergeant spoke for the troop and said, "Aw, this is that Indian with the paint horse. Come on, boys, she belongs here."

I looked for the stake that showed the numbers and finally found it in a brush pile way out of line.

I bet that bunch of Sooners already have the numbers for this place, I thought. The militia cleaned them out of the territory and told them not to come back till the run. I took the stake with the numbers to Alex and told him all that I knew. He pondered as we snaked ourselves back across the Cimarron to the mill. We didn't make it to Stillwater the first attempt, but in a few days we struck out north for a few miles and past the Yale Trading Post. We went to the Stillwater Land Office; we didn't go in but just spied out the location. The return trip was slow. Picking our way through the oak trees, we kept the course till we got north of Oilton and then slid right into the sawmill

We had church services the next morning at daylight. With Ole's singing and Alex's praying, all of us felt like we had worshiped the Lord that day. We slept till we couldn't. Sara had fixed a large pot of stew that fed us all day. The hot part of the day we all got in the spring pond and cooled off like water dogs.

Run of '93

Ole called a meeting under the park trees one morning and told all that he had been hearing from the wagon trains. The biggest mass of people was already at Arkansas City, Kansas, frothing at the bit to make the run. We planned to take the land numbers and be in Stillwater as soon as the land office opened that morning, getting in line and staying the course till we got registered. I was to ride Old Bob, Alex took an extra mule, and Sara was to pack food and water for the trip. Doc, Ole, Sara, and the boys were to take the wagons to the Cimarron River just across from the place we were to settle. As soon as we could get back, we would ford the river and make for our land. We knew we would have to have a show of force. Alex trained the boys to stay in the wagons out of sight with their guns ready to fire if necessary. They got out the Long Toms and fired off a few rounds without any shot, just lots of powder. I thought if we pull this off it would be a miracle.

PAT LORETT

Mill business stopped two days before the run; not one wagon came for lumber. Sara and I cooked extra bread and made plenty of butter and checked and rechecked the cook wagons. Alex had decided to leave all the farm equipment at the sawmill and take just two wagons and all the mules to pull across the Cimarron River. Ole said to take a long cable, for we might have trouble crossing with such heavy wagons. The morning of the fifteenth of September put Alex and me on a slow trail to Stillwater, keeping to the stands of oak trees. We saw plenty of people doing the same trick, but we guessed the militia was all at Arkansas City, Kansas. We made a cold camp that night and guessed that the cannon shot could be heard all over Indian Territory. We rode along with the traffic going into Stillwater and made the line, as it went over half-mile long. Alex got into the heaving, shoving line, and I kept him supplied with water and hard tack. I don't know how long we waited, but when he disappeared into the building I ran through my whole string of beads until he came out grinning like a coon! We backtracked to the wagons and found Ole, Sara, Doc, and the boys all set to cross the river. Ole had his long cable stretched out with a span of mules ready to swim the river; they wanted to cross over before dark! Alex rode on the first team, and almost immediately they had to swim for their lives. Just as the first team came out of water on the other side, two teams of mules set into motion, the large lumber wagon with cook wagon connected, and went into the water! The two wagons and teams fell away downstream as the team on the other side kept pulling them across. Three spans of mules and one hundred feet of cable stretched taunt pulled all our worldly goods right across the Cimarron River. Alex didn't stop; we rode that way all the way to my home. We were so tired by the time we made camp; Sara had a time getting any supper down us before we were snoring into the night air.

We tried to set up camp that first day but nothing seemed to work, Alex was exasperated with the way things were going. He called all of us to the stream below the spring, and we were told to take a bath, clothes and all! As it turned out, Alex was the biggest duck in the whole puddle, we air dried, and Ole and Alex proclaimed we were going to have church services out under a cottonwood tree. Ole started singing:

To God be the glory great things he has done,
So loved he the world he gave us his son.
Who yielded his life atonement for sin,
And opened the life gate that all may come in.
Praise the Lord, praise the Lord,
Let the earth hear his voice!
Praise the Lord, praise the Lord,
Let the people rejoice!
O come to the Father, thru Jesus the Son
And give Him the glory, great things he hath done.
Amen.

I could have stopped right there and had prayer, but my Alex proclaimed, "The Lord bless thee and keep thee: The Lord make his face shine upon thee and be gracious unto thee: The Lord lift up his countenance upon thee, and give thee peace. Amen and Amen."

The New Land

We all stood around and marveled at what the new land was beholding for us to see. After a quick sandwich, we fell over in the shade of the wagon and got a nap you wouldn't believe. We woke up to Alex and Ole building the first building on the new land—a six-by-six two-hole outhouse—downwind! We took the rest of the day off and planned what we had to do next.

Unload the wagons! We had to build a barn before winter. Build a corral to house the mules. I wanted a house built tomorrow! We needed to plow up a good big garden space for next spring.

They started on the first one and unloaded the lumber wagon. Alex dug a shallow hole, put the waterproof chest in the hole, and stacked all the lumber over it. I had missed the opportunity to ask Alex what was in the chest again. Ole and Sara started toward their home at the mill. I don't think they were out of sight when the gang of ruffians came over the hill, Old Bob came snorting into camp and let us know we had rough-looking company. The boys got their Long Toms loaded with power, their new lever-action rifles, and took up their places in the cook wagon. Doc got his new gun loaded with real shells, and we stood our ground as the leader started his tirade of belittlement.

Alex took just so much of that and then told him in no uncertain words that we had made the run and got this land. About that time the boys in the wagon put their guns out the slits, and you should have seen the whole bunch have doubts about causing trouble. It took Old Bob throwing a fit to set the gang back on its heels; he got a good bite of the backside of the ole leader. A six-gun shot rang out, and Old Bob squealed as he ran headlong into the center of the gang. All three Long Toms went off, and the smoke was so thick I couldn't see the bunch of ruffians leave the farm. Doc was so awestruck he never fired a shot; the boys had made up for the intrusion. We started to see blood on the ground; we checked everybody for that gunshot and found Old Bob bleeding from a neck wound. He had started his whimpering, and Doc and I tried to get a hold of him; that wounded horse didn't want anything to do with us. I crooned and his earlier training brought him to a standstill, foot, that plug just had a good headache from a grazed bullet. Doc and I got a long strip of cloth and some dry hay and bound his head like you would a sore tooth.

Ole and Sara came flying back into the camp, and I asked, "Why didn't you go on home?"

"Josie, what's going on? We heard shots."

We decided to have a cup of morning coffee and tell the tales. All of them looked so sheepishly and said the red Cimarron River was out of its banks! Lin spoke up. "We ran the robbers off, Old Bob has a sore tooth, Doc forgot to shoot, and here comes the Calvary!"

Alex shook his head and took charge of the militia. "You'll get down and have a cup of coffee while we get the battles sorted out."

That suited everybody, and we had our first real guest at my new home.

We told and retold about the scruffy bunch coming, giving us a hard time. The boys got their Long Toms and showed them the guns that ran the cowards off. The sergeant looked the Long Toms over, shook his head, and told Alex not to shoot them anymore, for the barrel was stopped up! Leo spoke with, "Oh, we don't put any shot in them. We poured the barrels full of black powder, jabbed a spit ball on top of the powder, and rammed it tight."

Sergeant spoke ever so quietly, asking the question of the day, "You mean you shot that gang with nothing but powder and wadding?"

"Yep," my youngest boy piped, "we shot one of them in the face!"

The whole troop beat each other on the back laughing. "Wait till we tell this at Stillwater, how a bunch of nester kids won the war of '93!"

The calvary mounted up and officially left two by two. Our whole group almost got our mouths sunburnt by standing there with them hung open. We tried to get back to work, but the calvary returned with the news that they had found a body down on the Cimarron River bank with a real deep bite in his rear end and all the flesh had been burnt off his face. The soldiers couldn't identify the old boy, but he was known to haul lumber from Pawnee.

"Oh, Alex, that was the man who gave the militia

such a bad time on the Pawnee trail." Lin chimed in with, "Yes, that was the man we shot in the face with the black power and wadding."

The militia all shook their heads at the tenacity of the homesteaders. They had taken the time to bury him and they guessed the case was closed. One of the soldier boys looked Old Bob over and said, "Sarge, let's get on the trail. These nesters have a horse all bound up like he has a sore tooth. Let's not mention that to the captain!"

Alex asked the sergeant if there was anyone else in that part of the run.

"There were very few, and the quarter south of us was vacant."

My husband scratched his jaw and spoke to me. "Josie, I think I will travel back with the unit and file on that south quarter for Joseph, my brother. I will take the wagon to Stillwater and maybe I can find some more iron for the barn. The calvary and Alex headed into Stillwater the next morning, and sure enough, he filed on the quarter section south of us, which gave us 320 acres in our name.

Alex didn't come in that night, but the next morning before noon here he came with a wagonload of pigs squealing their heads off for something to eat. Ole, Doc, and Alex right quick fastened a pigpen out of the barn boards. I looked it all over and told the boys to take buckets and pick up all the acorns they could find down by the river. As soon as we could get some woven wire put up, we could let those porkers find their own feed. They no sooner let the hogs out till I could hear the penned chickens wanting out. Alex had really had a find coming back from Stillwater. A chicken pen with house connected came next with a few nests for eggs.

By the next morning we had three eggs! I mixed a big batch of pancakes with those three eggs, and we ate the last of the butter and milk. I reminded Alex that he took the wagon to Stillwater to get iron for the barn. He smirked that all-knowing look and said, "Josie, in the morning let's kill that biggest shoat for us some fatback and have a pot of beans when I get back from taking Ole and Sara home."

I winked back and said, "You go ahead and take the company back to their house, and I'll get the fatback that we need." I set a big iron pot of beans to soak that night just before I almost died of exhaustion.

Makin' Do

Doc, the boys, and I butchered the shoat the next morning while Alex took Ole and Sara home. Alex returned at noon to pork and beans with hot cornpone fried over the open fire. We had plenty of fresh spring water, and old Jerz decided she would go dry. This left us with no milk for the boys or for cornbread. We had another cow, but she was with calf so we made do just like we were on the trail—we did without! The pigs were in constant need of acorns, so Alex let them loose to wonder the sandhills to find whatever they could eat. Alex brought the farm machinery back from Ole's, got out the turning plow, and plowed a good-sized garden space. Huge mistake—the hogs took to rooting all the plowed ground like hogs like to do. Alex scratched his jaw and said, "Oh well, the ground got fertilized by the hogs."

Alex got to plow again, and again, and about the third time we had more hogs than when we started rooting out the holes. Alex got the boys around him and said, "Boys, we got some big hogs coming to our garden spot. Let's take the guns and get us our winter meat!"

The first day they killed a big sow, field dressed, and hung the carcass in a tree. Alex told the boys, "We need a couple of smaller ones to make it through the winter. A red one and a spotted one soon hung in the same tree we called the hog tree. I got out my stone crocks and put two boys grinding sausage by the tubful, two more who could stir the iron pot, and we rendered that big old sow down into lard. We spent two days frying sausage into patties; put them down in the stone crock covered with hot, salty grease. I wasn't satisfied until we had four eight-gallon crocks completely full of sausage.

I was getting low on supplies by this time, so Doc and I took a wagon, three boys, and Old Bob to the Yale Trading Post. We were able to make Yale before noon and tied up to the trading post. A fine young man greeted us and said his name was Mays.

"What can I do for you? Have you got anything that I can buy, trade, or sell? What is your name? Whoa, what will you take for that spotted Indian pony?"

I finally got a word in edgewise and stated I needed a bill filled, and no Old Bob was not for sale.

"Ma'am, what do people call you?"

"My name is Josephine Lorett, and this is my doctor, and my three sons are called Lin, Laurence, and Leo. We homesteaded 320 acres out east and south by the Cimarron River."

"Ma'am, let me have your bill, and while I'm filling it you scout through my whole post and see what else you need."

My family looked at everything they had as Dahl May filled our wagon. Dahl came up with almost everything that I had on the list except some hinges that Alex wanted for the barn doors.

"Ma'am, is there anything else you need? If'n you don't have enough money, I can carry you till your crop comes in."

I corrected him and said, "You can call me Josie but not 'ma'am'! If I don't have enough money, we will have to leave something out!"

"Yes, ma—okay, Josie. I appreciate your honesty, but we all have hard times once in a while."

"Dahl, what do you to trade for?"

"Josie, I just started this trading post a month ago, and I will buy or trade for anything that people can eat. Do you have any meat of any kind?" I started to tell him about the hogs we had butchered but let that slide. Alex needed to talk to Dahl May and make that deal. Doc and I felt it best that we get settled up and head for home. I did buy some crackers and cheese to eat on the way home.

We spent my whole twelve dollars and just got the wagon full, I thought. Alex had supper warmed up as we pulled into the yard with Ole Bob about worn out pulling all that distance. We ate more crackers and cheese with warmed soup and plenty of spring water. I told Alex about Dahl May wanting to trade for any kind of fresh meat. My sweet husband smiled and nodded. I could just see him wanting all kinds of iron for that blacksmith shop.

Alex, Doc, and the boys worked on the barn as long as the days had daylight. They had to go back into town for more hardware and stayed much too long. I kept looking for the wagon, but it took Old Bob to hear the

traces jingling with a wagon full of supplies. The barn
went up with lots of work by all involved. I tried to
help, but the cooking took full time.

I cured the remaining hogs, and we had all the meat
we wanted. As the roof went on I noticed a pipe sticking out the top.

"What is that for, Alex?" I asked.

He shrugged his shoulders and said, "To let the hot
air out."

The barn took on a real permanent look as the
doors hid the inside, and there were even windows on
two sides. I asked what those were for, and he told me
again they were for letting the hot air out. Another
trip into the Yale Trading Post brought a wagon full
of more lumber and flooring for the hayloft. I didn't
discover the black cast iron cookstove covered up with
more lumber. The menfolk worked all morning putting
that stove together and connecting it to the stovepipe
in the top of the roof. The first thing I knew there was
smoke coming out of the pipe, and I thought, *Fire!*
Those men had installed a new wood-burning cookstove in the barn! I busied myself around and stepped
into the first barn-house in Indian Territory.

First Winter

We got a frost before we moved into the barn-house, which put the whole gang in the moving mode. We had spread our bed under the wagons as usual, went to bed with our clothes on, covered up with all the blankets and my buffalo robe, and about froze up. We were so stiff by daylight I barely made it in the house to build a roaring fire in the cookstove. The boys trailed in one at a time wrapped in a blanket, and we sat around on the floor trying to warm up. The menfolk decided we best hurry and get the house closed up before the snow drifted through the cracks. Each day it became easier to heat and cook. I got my sourdough starter going again, and we had bread every meal.

Our spare cow was not broke to milk but a good understanding about sweet feed got us plenty to drink. We sat all the cured meat in the cook wagon, and it kept the whole winter. The boys killed a big turkey for thanksgiving. I got all kinds of bulbs out of the spring,

PAT LORETT

we would have liked some sweet potatoes, but we acted like we were still on the trail and did without. Word came over the river that Ole and Sara wanted us to come for Thanksgiving I packed all our food and loaded the wagon completely full of people, food, blankets, and off we went. The river was almost completely dry so we rode across on the rocky bottom Sara and Ole greeted us like grandparents. We spread all the food out on the tables, and we grazed on the best fare all day long. Ole led the singing, Alex told of Thanksgivings past, and we praised the Lord as one happy family. We were so full coming home that every bounce made us wonder why we had eaten so much. The kids covered up with the blankets, we wondered where Doc had gotten to. We found him in with the kids snoring with that silly smile on his face.

Doc began looking peaked before Christmas. I tried all my home remedies, and as Sara had said, he didn't last very long. I found him one morning sitting up against the cookstove; I guessed he was trying to keep warm. Alex made him a wooden box where I laid him out. Doc was a full-blood Asakiwaki Indian, but his people had all died in the oppression back east we pondered whether to give him a full Indian burial or a white man's. Alex took me over to Sara, and we asked each other the question, all we could do was shake our heads. We finally went over to the Indian camp of the Sac and Fox. We met with the elders, and they pondered the problem. Finally they said, "Yes, we will give the old healer a burial."

A few days later we took the coffin with Doc laid out so nice back to the Sac and Fox camp on the hill. As we neared the settlement, we drove by the above-ground burial grounds of countless braves. Yes, there was a new stand without a body on it. I met with the elders and said again that I wanted to put Doc up on his last resting place; they agreed if their medicine man could go along and say the last word. We undressed ole Doc and tied him above ground for his final reward. I don't remember what the medicine man said, but it was cold, and I'm sure he kept it short. I counted my beads around and said, "Dust to dust," for my final words. We remembered old Doc for years to come, how he had helped me get through a very difficult time; we tried to count the children that he had brought into the world, how many he had lost. The list went on without end. I praised the Lord that I had gotten to know him, especially in his last years.

We got snowed in with nothing to do but count our blessings. Alex had been working out in the blacksmith shop, and he called us to come help him and said to put on plenty of clothes. As we drew near the shop, I found my Old Bob harnessed up and standing so patiently. Alex came and told the family to cover all our eyes and guess what he had in the shop. I couldn't think of what in the world could cheer us up. He opened the main door and showed us a brand new sled that all of us could ride in! Alex had tried to hook Old Bob to the sled, but he was not going to stand still for that. I crooned and that old plug backed right between the staves. We piled on and took the first sleigh ride around the farm. Fun!

We spent the day going a thousand miles with my Old Bob supplying the power. I turned him loose, we came in for dinner, and the warm cookstove dried us to the skin. I had cooked beans the night before and right quick filled our bellies with beans from the pot. The boys wanted to get right back into the sled, but the three youngest and I needed our rest. We bunked up in our beds and slept till dark.

Alex had cut a cedar tree, so we set it up and decorated with popcorn strings and some clam shells that we'd found in the spring. The Bible story was Luke the second chapter that Lin read so nice. We exchanged hugs all around and wished each other a Merry Christmas and a Happy New Year.

"Alex, I need a drying shed for my herbs that I'm going to plant this spring." All I got from that German descendant was a grunt.

"Alex?"

"Hmm, yes, Josie. I was a plannin'. How big?"

"We need a root cellar to store all kinds of winter vegetables, a cellar to hide from the windstorms, a smokehouse to cure a lot of meat."

"Wait, Josie, that's all too much!"

"Yes, that's right, it is too much, but if we have two more boys we will need a lot of space."

"Oh, Josie, are we going to have more sons?"

"Alex, my dear husband, best you get to building and let the Lord give the increase!"

He went off in the wrong direction muttering, "Maybe we should have stayed in Missouri!" He only made it to the outhouse and came right back in.

"Josie, let's you and me take a walk out to my blacksmith shop. I want to show you something."

I changed to my outside apron, grabbed a head wrap, and followed his bent-over shuffle.

"Josie, I need to go back to Braymer, Missouri," he confided.

"Oh no, Alex, let's leave that place forever. I never want to go back!"

"Josie, you didn't understand me. I need to go back

to Braymer on business. Sweet Josie, I will leave you here with two of the boys and their guns, take the other three with me, and be back in a couple of months. You won't have to face the militia. Just stay right here, work the boys clearing trees, planting garden, tending your herbs. I will be back as soon as I can sell the tree farm. Now, Josie, I want to show you something that I have been moving since we left Ole's."

I peered in to an almost empty waterproof chest; there was only one layer of ten-dollar gold pieces left!

"Oh, Alex, I wanted to know what was in that chest every time I saw it."

"Yes, Joise, I didn't tell you on purpose if we had been robbed, I didn't want you to be tortured."

"Oh, Alex, I love you so much, but what if they tortured you?"

Alex put on his most stubborn German look, pouched out his lip, and stated, "I would never tell anything!"

I thought, *I bet that is true,* as Alex connected the slip and started digging me a bigger root cellar. As it turned out, he had enough lumber to build a smokehouse beside the root cellar. The whole project was completed before spring brought the cool rains.

First Plantin' of the New Land

Alex left me here with my gun-shooting boys and their new lever-action guns. Our boys were so proud of their prowess with that old flint lock gun; they hung it over the door to prove wars of years past. Alex had plowed the garden space again after we put up a hog-tight fence. Porkers visited each night to do their rooting thing, our fence held, and we got on with planting a huge garden. I found a glade to plant my herbs, a spot close to a hog wallow to plant some Sang. Our stock came out of the winter kind of thin, and they wondered the countryside looking for anything green. Alex had taken three teams of mules with him, one wagon, three boys with their new guns, and, of course, his empty waterproof chest.

I had kind of forgotten about our Indian neighbors until one morning before dawn, I heard their ponies stomp the ground. I wondered what they had brought me. I made them wait until the coffee was made then put on my most stern look and stepped out on the porch. There were six with one riding double. I signed for them to get down and have some coffee; they never stirred, just let the extra rider down on the ground, turned on their heels, and left the way they came, silently. I stepped up to the brave and got a morning shock. A very small girl looked out from under her shawl with those coal-colored eyes; the eyes clouded over and pain came with a low groan. I quickly examined her and couldn't find anything wrong. I started to help her inside my barn-house, and those eyes flashed her fear of living in a house. I thought, *Oops, this outside human will want to stay under the wagons with the animals.*

I helped her to lie down under the tent, and she tightened her grip on my arm and groaned louder.

This woman-child can't be left to suffer so, I reasoned. *You don't suppose she is in labor?*

I examined her again and, sure enough, had been for some time. I wished for Doc right then; that old gent would know when to operate. I needed to get her to relax and maybe I could help her. Some of my herbs in coffee did the trick, my crooning put her to sleep, and I was able to determine that the baby was way too premature to ever live.

But we must try! I thought.

Her sleep was a good cure for the anxious trials of life, and I could get my thread to tie the cord off. I got us more coffee and thought, *Now is as good a time as any.* I delivered that squeaking baby girl to a very cruel, cold world. Her baby squeaks woke the small woman, and I could tell right away she was not going to have anything to do with a baby that small. I called my boy

Lin to milk our cow and maybe, just maybe, we could buy some time.

The tiny baby girl was hungry and immediately tried to suck anything close to her mouth. I spooned warm milk into her mouth, and Tiny One got her first milk. Yes, that's what I named the sweet little girl-child. I could completely hide her with one hand. I didn't notice her mother watching with black eyes, and she wouldn't let me know what she was thinking. I signed to the mother, and she spoke to me in my own language; her Indian name was Little Elf. I had found another Indian who spoke English! I didn't let on the child was white with brown eyes but started that crooning sound, and Little Elf settled down to wanting to hold her child. I was thrilled and had some hope for the day.

Tiny One woke soon and squeaked, "Feed me time." Little Elf immediately gave me the baby back and told me she didn't have any milk!

"Oh, Little Elf, we can fix that. Let's get you some warm milk, breakfast, and we'll soon be in production."

I could see Little Elf didn't believe me, but breakfast did sound good.

Little Elf and I grinned that all-knowing look, and I could see us women had hope for the future. We fed Tiny One all the cow's milk she wanted and, just like any baby, instant sleep. We made it through the first day without any milk from the new mother; she would hold Tiny One to her breast but nothing. I realized Little Elf needed more water and lots more milk we fed the mother each time the baby took on cow's milk. It was into the second day when Little Elf came to me with milk flowing down the front of her garment. We fed Tiny One all the mother's milk she wanted, and we had one happy baby. Lin and Leo took their turn holding this tiny girl-child, their thumbnail was the size of her hand. Little Elf strengthened, and I said something about her going back to her man.

"No! I can't go anywhere. I don't have a man. He died this winter. I can't go back. Don't make me!"

"Now, now, Little Elf, you don't have to go back if you don't want to. Let's get settled down and we'll see what works out."

Little Elf just couldn't hold her turmoil any longer and told me the sad story about her life. Her parents were well-to-do with a large plantation in Tennessee, with slaves and holdings. The resettlement of all Indians completely wiped out the estate, put the residents in poverty, and made them walk to Oklahoma. Her folks had died on the way, and she had married a good, strong half-breed. He was killed by the militia, and she soon found out she was with child. She had settled on the south side of the Cimarron River with a band of Cherokees. She or her child never seemed to grow, but at the end of her term several of the braves decided to take her to a healer.

They brought Little Elf to me, and I was involved with an Indian tribe again.

ON WITH LIFE

Alex had been gone less than a week. We had more planting to do, I had an extra mouth to feed, and the bottom fell out of the sky. Little Elf got over her fear of living in our barn-house, and I discovered that she was a good cook, worker, and, most of all, a planter! We worked around the rain and got all our seed planted in short order. Our new hog-tight fence had been breached, and we found the biggest sow rooting down the corn rows with her long nose. Old Bob had come to the barn-house and let me have his eerie feeling; I surveyed the garden and could see more meat. Lin got out his new 30–30, took good aim, and missed. Oh well, so much for big slabs of bacon. We fixed the fence, and Little Elf noticed blood on the ground and took off like she knew what she was doing. She traveled some distance and came back with the biggest smile you could have imagined. We hooked the sled onto Old Bob, and he pulled all of us to a huge pile of hog. All we could do was walk around all that meat but couldn't figure out how to get it back to our barn-house. Again Little Elf solved the problem with a big knife and an axe. She quartered all five hundred pounds of hog, and we were able to stow our summer's meat on the sled. Little Elf took over the hog, and we helped her render all the hog fat down into my sausage crocks. I sugar cured the hams, shoulders, and bacon. The new smokehouse was stuffed to the rafters with that old fat sow. We started the new smokehouse to smoking with a small leaf fire. As the house heated up, we put on more leaves and oak wood. I would open the door and check to see if the meat was hot enough. We kept the smoking going for three days till all the meat was a good dark color and left it to be used as needed.

Tiny One was the main attraction around Lin and Leo, but she needed her mother come mealtime. More rain brought on the weeds, and our days were filled with trying to nurture the garden. I checked on my herb glade, and we had to weed it also. I lost track of the time and wondered how my Alex was doing with selling the tree farm, making sure that the boys were all well, and watching out for the trail robbers. I just had to turn it all over to the Lord and pray for them daily.

We started to find pinecones in the barn-house, in the smokehouse, the root cellar, then I lost my beads with a pinecone offering in their place.

"Okay, who stole my beads?"

To me the whole lot looked guilty as sin, we turned the barn-house inside out, and all we found were more pinecones. Little Elf and I looked at each other and found that all-knowing smirk on each other. We gathered the boys together for a family counsel and told them about Mr. Pack Rat. How he was a sneak-Pete, trader, borrower, collector, always stored food for winter, and then the worst trait, he traveled at night. We decided to look around the campsite for anything that was out of place or bigger than normal. We looked till suppertime to no avail; all we had was hunger. Little Elf took over and fixed us fry bread with some kind of watery soup after a couple of helpings all around, the boys and I decided we would last till breakfast. Elf didn't say much after supper; she just took Tiny One and disappeared into the woods.

Well, the little Indian maid is getting her confidence back, I thought.

She came back in with her all-knowing grin. I took one look and knew she was up to something. Finally she shared her version of Mr. Pack Rat.

"Grandma Josie, I think that rat is coming a long way off I walked way over on that hill and found a pine tree with not many cones on the ground, and I think his mound is on the other side of the hill. He comes by the pine tree, gets his gift, and comes running to the barn-house."

We put everything up that night except a small ball of yarn with a long tail. All of us slept like logs, and, sure enough, in the morning the ball of yarn was gone and a fresh pine cone was in its place. I could see the boys were ready for a good pack rat hunt after breakfast. Little Elf wanted to take the wagon to haul all the plunder back to the barn-house.

I thought, *Josie, that Little Elf is a thinker.*

We got Old Bob harnessed to the farm wagon, and I noticed all Little Elf took was a throwing stick. Of course, the boys took their guns. We put Tiny One on her carrying board, and off we went to hunt rats. I hoped that Alex wouldn't come back and see all this going on.

The rat safari wound up farther than Little Elf thought, but that big mound of black oak sticks soon came into view. We walked around and around that nest, and when one of the boys spied the tail of yarn we knew we had the right rat nest!

Almost immediately Little Elf called the boys together and said the worst words, "Let's take this nest apart stick by stick and haul it all to the barn-house for cookstove wood."

"Oh foot! More work," the boys said as one.

I reasoned that the Indian girl had a head on her shoulders! We loaded that nest stick by stick into the wagon, following the tail of yard to the innermost nest. The boys had forgotten all about their guns but were hot on the trail. Little Elf got her throwing stick and stood at the ready out beside the wagon. Wasn't long before the biggest long-tailed rat sprung from his nest and made for parts unknown. Little Elf swung side-armed, and that throwing stick found its mark not twenty yards away. All we could do was look dumb-founded with our mouths hung open. Little Elf walked to her kill, picked it up by the tail, and said, "This one will be about the right size," as she stowed her prize under the wagon seat.

We told the boys to start picking up the nuts and seeds in the nest. That rat had been storing up for a hard winter till he started trading from us. We picked up until we were tired and then picked up some more. My string of beads was in a cute little nest with some shiny nails, staples, and two ten-dollar gold pieces. *Alex left his waterproof chest open!* I thought.

We started in earnest searching out the rest of the

nest. When we were satisfied, Little Elf came with a cotton sack, and we saved all the nest material for kindling. You could hardly tell there had ever been a nest there by the time we were through. My boys and I learned a good lesson that day: There can be good come out of every experience.

We went home and unloaded all the black oak sticks in our woodpile, stored the nuts in the root cellar, and I fixed the biggest mess of pancakes, sausage, and fresh milk, while Tiny One got her dinner. We feasted on the bounty of the land, gave the Lord credit, and napped the afternoon away. I awoke to the sounds of a crooning Indian girl; she had skinned that pack rat, stretched the hide on a piece of bark, and was combing its hair with my comb! I started to pitch a fit but thought better of it, if that rat ever needed a friend it was now. The boys were so curious, and all Little Elf would say was, "You will see," as she stowed the hide up in the rafters of the smoke shed.

First School in Indian Territory

Most of the families that made the run of '93 had a whole string of kids. A spot in the southeast corner of our land housed the Roosevelt School. The river benders hired a school marm for the 1894–1895 school year, and Alex and I housed her with us in the barn-house. I had another woman in our house, and she was from back east somewhere. My boys had missed two years of school during the trek from Braymer, Missouri. Miss Adlie soon won their trust, and they caught up with their grades. There was always a spelling bee, ciphering, contest of the times tables, or listing of the capitols of the states.

In the land run of '89, Guthrie was set aside as the capitol of Oklahoma. Miss Adlie added the new capitol to her list and homeschooled her young charges. I grew to love her eastern ways and the lilt of her voice. The way Miss Adlie said "Nu Yook City" was quite a hoot.

Curious about my ancestry, she asked why I had

such high cheek bones. I opened up and told her the complete story of the Indian oppression in Missouri, whip scars and all! Miss Adlie stood over me and held my head to her bosom and we cried together. I confided that I was over all that and had forgiven my oppressors; she said she was sorry that old wounds had been opened and asked my forgiveness. It was my turn to hold her sobbing body to me, and we both cried ourselves out. The bond we made that day lasted a lifetime for both of us, and I found a real friend.

The school flourished as Miss Adlie won the confidence of the river benders. In fact, the first year she gave out high school diplomas to four students to start Oklahoma A&M College at Stillwater. I counted fifty-four kids in twelve grades the third year it was open. Miss Adlie used the upper classes to teach until we could hire extra teachers. How she accomplished all that is a wonder, but she said it was a labor of love that pushed them along. The homesteaders all had the same purpose; get the schools up and running and the land would be proved up in good time.

LIFE

We filled the drying sheds completely full of beans, corn, squash, seeds, and herbs that first year. The crows had found our garden and had come to feast in our buffet. Our scarecrow in overalls made Little Elf smile, as she fashioned her owl down close to the spring, we had crows by the cloud full. The boys got out their .22 rifle, and we had all kinds of crow stew! I don't know how much we ate, but the stew pot was kept full. As the saying went, "Dig deep, the crow is in the bottom of the pot!"

We didn't lack for something to do. I think it was Old Bob that came with his snorting and neighing right at dark. I knew we were to have company before breakfast the next morning. Little Elf and I started cooking early. I sat sourdough bread; the stew pot was cleaned with a fresh pot of crow and beans. We all took a spring cold bath and changed clothes.

I felt Alex was on his way, and we had to be ready

before daylight if I knew him! True to his nature, Old Bob heard those trace chains clanging right at the crack of dawn, Alex's mules started their heehaw game, as Old Bob charged around the homestead countless times. Alex and another man sitting up front with my precious boys ganged up on the very top of two wagons. We all hugged till we were tired, cried till we couldn't cry anymore, then Alex's brother Joseph made his appearance. I started all over again! Little Elf stayed in the barn-house and let us have the moment; she had the beans cooking and breakfast ready when we stormed in hungry as hounds. I tried to introduce them all around but was at a loss for words. I finally told them I had delivered Little Elf about two months ago. Alex raised his eyebrows, the boys got Tiny One out, and we savored the day of reunion. I asked what the lumber was for in the wagons; the menfolk just looked blank and didn't say a word. I just knew something awful had happened. I kept asking questions, and Alex told me I would know when all when the wagons were unloaded. I was ready to start right in but did ask about Ole and Sara. Joseph spoke up and told me that they were fine and they would be over in a few days. I wanted to know everything at once, but the telling took much longer. We fed them the entire crow soup that we had fixed; they said it tasted good but was sure tough!

Alex and Joseph made a large place to pile the new lumber so it would cure, and out came a coffin-shaped box. I treed this box and could just see more lumber. There were holes in the top. They opened the box and there were fruit trees of all different kinds from Braymer, Missouri, packed in wet sawdust. I had to cover my face and cried out, "Oh, Alex, did you bring me some russets, wine saps, and some of those Arkansas blacks?" I was overwhelmed with thoughts of a real orchard on our farm. My dear Alex held me and said the most comforting words, "Josie, I want you to have all the fruit we can ever use from these trees." I thought, *Yes, I bet he does; now I wonder who will take care of this orchard.*

We started right in the next morning planting those seedlings; much to my relief, we finished before dark. I wondered that night, *Will we ever have everything planted we want?*

Ole and Sara came over and spent the weekend with us. It was so good to talk our yarns out. Sara looked Tiny One over and told Little Elf she was sure a pretty baby but needed to grow faster. We decided the baby needed some growing pills. Little Elf smirked her lips and looked the other way as she spoke.

"You made mention about Tiny One being small, I was small when I was born, and my parents let me be and I grew to this size by the time I was twelve years old."

Sara and I nodded, let things be, and Little Elf continued. "I went full term with Tiny One, and Grandma Josie helped me get back my confidence. I think it's about time for me to go back across the river and join my tribe."

I looked things over and told Little Elf that if I could help her, she could always come to my home on the west side of the Cimarron River. We packed her meager belongings, and I gave her my buckskins (they had gotten too tight on me!).

I sent Little Elf home on Old Bob and told her to let him go and he would come back. Old Bob swelled with pride as soon as I put an Indian blanket on his back; he knew just what to do. I handed Little Elf a single rope bridle, and off went Old Bob with his precious cargo. Tiny One looked so cute with her new pack rat cap stretched over her head. The boys went out shaking, their heads talking about putting a rat cap on. I didn't tell them that there was a tail on the back that hung all the way to Little One's knees. I stated before, that was my entrance into the Indian tribes around me. Yes, I was midwife to many an Indian baby in the middle of the night and was never rewarded so much. I tried to outgive the tribes, but they always made sure we were well taken care of. Old Bob came back the next day with a dream catcher tied on the side of his head. I very carefully placed it in a box and had a remembrance of delivering a mixed race child back in '94.

White House on Yon Hill

Alex and Joseph built a round granary to hold the corn crop up off the ground. I looked it over and made a deal for a momma cat and three kittens to control the mice and rats. I remembered the waterproof chest and asked Alex where our money was stashed. His reply was short and to the point, "Josie, come with me and I'll show you your life's savings as of today."

We walked to the blacksmith's shop, and I thought, *You don't suppose he has hidden the chest in plain sight!*

"Here, Josie, is our complete estate in this box." I opened it to find nothing but a wreath of business papers.

"Alex, I knew it. You have lost all our money!"

"Now, now, Josie. I did the best I could, but times are hard and we're not settled yet."

The first document was sale of the tree farm in Missouri; the next was a deposit slip from the Stillwater Territorial Bank where Alex had moved our account awaiting our instructions. A large roll of papers came out next from an architect in Braymer, Missouri.

"Alex, what are all these drawings? It looks like a large house."

"Yes, that's right, sweet Josie. On the next page are the bedrooms that will be upstairs. If you will look at the stack of lumber under the tarps, you will see part of the house that Ole will be sawing."

"Sweet Josie, we're going to be able to build a large house up on yon hill that will house all seven boys at one time!"

"Oh, Alex, we just have five boys—oh! I understand!"

The men folk harvested our corn patch and stowed the complete crop in the new corn crib. Our cats took up residence under the corn and went right to their jobs of riding the farm of varmints. Alex and I staked out the house on the hill and wished the house was already finished, like yesterday! Joseph and Alex built a barn-house on the south quarter that was reserved for Joseph and his bride-to-be. We went into the winter with full larders of food; I kept us healthy for the most part. We had a spell of whooping cough that left us weak as kittens; my home-made black cough syrup either cured us or scared the cold away. I was so tired of the winter; I wished to go directly into summer.

Joseph decided he needed to go back to Braymer, Missouri, to see his sweetheart; he took a wagon and two spans of mules and enough food to get there. Alex and I wondered what was up, but that was their decision to make. Ole and Sara came over for Christmas and spent the holidays with us. We were starved for somebody else to talk to, and Sara and I did our share. The boys wanted to do the Christ child play so with the help of the menfolk we made a manger out on the back porch, and Ole sang "Away in the Manger"; we joined in on the last verse to help him through the complete song.

Sara made us a big pot of taffy, and we played ourselves out pulling. We ate so much our tongues were sore from the exercise. Ole had shut the mill down until after the first of the year, so the mill hands could be with their families. We had a family meeting and decided to stay up until the New Year came in. Ole had brought his pocket watch with him, so we had the time. As the New Year came in, most of us were sleeping like a bunch of hogs (all in one heap!) Next day Alex, Ole, and all the boys set up the saddle anvil on a stump outside of the blacksmith shop, filled the square hole full of black powder and a long fuse. They took a horn anvil and sat it on top of the loaded hole. We celebrated the New Year with the ringing of the anvils. How many people heard the blast we didn't know, but the sound carried to Yale six miles away. I suppose that was the first time all the nesters had heard the ringing of the anvils on New Year's Eve. Ole and Sara took their leave the next morning with us promising to visit them next.

The rains brought two surprises: time to plant garden, and Joseph came with all his furniture and a new bride named Annie. She was so lovely, young, and I had another woman to talk to! We started her household chores the first day with setting sourdough bread to rise overnight, and we baked it off for the noon meal. By this time we had nine mouths to feed three meals a day, so the bread-making was every third day. Joseph and Annie started their housekeeping in their barn-house just like Alex and I had almost a year ago. Both gardens got planted early and promptly froze out. "*Humph,*" was all we could say as we replanted the second time. Having two families so close solved the labor problem; we just combined our projects and the work expanded.

Old Bob took his turn making a fuss one evening that old boy took to running around the barn-house at full tilt. We went on alert! The boys got their guns loaded and spent the rest of the day looking and listening. I went out to soothe the beast, and he nibbled my arm so hard he brought blood. I thought, *Who is coming?*

We tried to sleep, but Old Bob wasn't to have anything like that.

"Okay, Bob, I'm comin'." I led him to my get aboard stump for mounting and let him have his head. He bounced me around so much, I thought I hadn't been riding enough. He crossed the river and carried me to a campsite in the distance. I hollered some distance away but never got an answer. The fire was about out, and I was really being cautious. I looked the rig over, and then it hit me: *This wagon belongs to Sam and Nella!* I heard this pitiful wail come on the wind; I realized the family was sick.

Sam crawled out from under the wagon. I hardly recognized him he was so thin. I sat on Old Bob as Sam told me not to get down; they had the sickness, and I might catch it. I asked Sam what he felt like.

"Josie, don't come any closer. All my family has got specks on us, high fever; we're out of food and water!"

I asked him again what the specks looked like.

"Oh, Josie, they are little knots with white heads and itch like crazy."

I circled downwind and sniffed the air. "Oh, Sam, your family has got chicken pox. I know you feel bad,

but I'll send for my bag and we'll have you fixed up in
no time."

I fixed a note on old Bob and told Alex to bring my
bag of herbs, food, and water enough for a few days.
It wasn't long before there came my surrey with all I
wanted. Alex took Sam's team to our house and left
me to get them well. Food with some of my plant gel
put the whole bunch to snoring. I made camp, and it
was then I realized Sam and Nella had starved out in
Guthrie. All they had were the clothes on their backs;
they were so thin I had thoughts of the chills taking
their lives. I tried to find their little girl and feared the
worst as I doctored the remaining four. Alex brought
over fresh milk daily, and I soon had the pox drying
up. I stayed with the family for a week, then Old Bob
pulled the wagon to our barn-house. Alex and I took
Sam's family in for the duration until they could decide
what to do.

Sam and Nella strengthened with the coming days,
and I had three women to talk to by then. Annie was a
wonderful worker and came most every day for another
recipe to cook for her Joseph. Sam started right in working his heart out for Alex, and we caught the spring
planting craze. More corn ground was broke out, land
cleared for a hay meadow, and corrals for the mules.
Alex and Sam went to Yale for supplies and came back
with a white donkey. I didn't ask any questions, but I
could see that stud the father of a whole string of white
mules!

Sam's family cleared of the pox, and we heard the
whole story of them going to Guthrie in the spring of
'93. They made the run but came up empty-handed.
Sam had worked some to keep the family together, but
most of the homesteaders had the same problem: no

resources, nothing to eat, no place to work, and on and on. Sam decided to go back to Missouri and start all over again. Nelliene, their girl,got the chicken pox first and had died on the trail; they didn't even remember where the grave was. The pox spread to the rest of the family; they ran out of food, water, and time. Old Bob had found them on the riverbank; he came and got me out of bed, and I could see the plight they were in. I thought, *I bet this story has been played out many a time among the Oklahoma homesteaders.*

Ole and Sara heard about Sam's family and brought what blankets they could spare. We killed another wild hog, cured the whole carcass, and made the menfolk enough bean soup to last a week.

HOUSE RAISIN'

Alex got that itchy feeling about the house not going up and hired Sam to head up the construction. The word got out in Yale that we were going to build a large house, and we had carpenters come out of the wood-work. Nesters who got their crops laid by took turns helping with the project. Construction went on for two years with I don't know how many workers coming and going. A gang of brick masons came in from Mexico and dug the biggest hole beside the back porch. I asked Alex what the hole was for, and he told me a cistern. I didn't have the courage to ask him what that was for until they started hauling bricks from the rail yard in Stillwater. Sam was sure a wonder being the head boss of the job; his string of laborers brought sandstone blocks from the river bluff and laid them in the very bottom of the cistern. Then lots of concrete held them all together, with the bottom covered with bricks laid just right to hold the weight of the bowl. Thirty feet higher the bowl was capped off with a huge concrete slab the height of the back porch. Plaster was mixed by the wagonload for several days, and the inside of the cistern became just like a stone crock glaze. The last trip from Stillwater brought all the chain, buckets, cistern head, and cover to be installed.

Sam got that faraway look toward the Cimarron River. Here he had been with us for some months, and he had not got to go fishing. All the menfolk who were working on the house decided to take some time off to visit their families and to celebrate Independence Day. The men decided to go home and bring their families back, camp out on the hillside, catch enough fish to feed everybody, and shoot the anvils off. We all buckled down to the task, and by the time the fourth came around we were in high sprits. We invited the whole river bend area to come and celebrate with us. Ole and Sara came early and told the story of a preacher that had come through their park earlier in the spring of 1892. They were sure he had settled down on the Cimarron River on some school land.

Sam stepped forward and said, "Let's have a preaching at daylight the morning of the fourth then have a fish fry on the land of Alex and Josephine Lorett."

That sounded great to the menfolk, so Ole went on over to the homestead of William H. Fritch and they all agreed to have early church services that day if Ole would lead the singing.

I started writing the names down as they came; Lundays, Queers, Fritches, Stoops, Prestons, Boltons, Wells, Kerbys, Rosses, Ricks, Coys, Loretts, Reeds, Roushes, Pences, Dilleys ... I'm sure I missed some, but we all met before daylight and sang those songs that are forever. William H. Fritch finished up his sermon in time to start the fat frying for the first celebration on that side of the river bend area. Sam and a lot of men had come from the river with a wagonload of flathead catfish they had noodled. We fried enough fish that morning to feed the whole community, and then the men folk got ready to ring the anvils. They had already set the saddle anvil on its big stump, primed it with powder and a fuse, and set the horned anvil on top. The people stood way back they were not prepared for the first explosion, and the anvil went out of sight and came back down and buried itself in the dirt. A huge applause brought on a complete series of explosions. The talk of the community meeting held at the Loretts', singing, preaching, fish frying, and the fireworks, all held July 4, 1899.

After thirty days of curing the cistern, it was back filled to the very top with dirt the men had dug out. All this was going on while the house was receiving the second story. I will never forget the day the last of the cedar shingles went on the roof; our house was dried in. Yes, I said *our home*. I couldn't claim it to be my own home now.

My Alex worked right alongside the workers; he had to rely on the boys to do the farming. They may have not done as good a job farming as Alex wanted, but the corn crib was full after corn-shucking time. I soon got hungry and remembered to keep fixing meals.

I'll never forget the day the painters came and painted the outside of the house in one day. The primer coat was mixed on the farm from thirty-gallon barrels of white lead and linseed oil. Painters with big brushes seemed to slop that primer all over the nice boards. By the next morning it was a smooth as silk. Another two coats of brilliant white took my breath away.

I didn't go inside until all the plastering was done, and that made it look ready for me to move in. "No, no, my Josie," said Alex "we're going to trim the inside with white oak that Ole has sawn, shaped, and sanded in his sawmill." Another crew of trim carpenters came this time, and, boy, were they good. Every joint had to be just right or Sam would make them work till he couldn't stick a piece of paper between the joints.

The day Sam came with his cabinet maker, and we laid out the upper and lower cabinets was a day to remember. Ole had outdone himself with huge, wide slabs of white oak to make all the doors and cabinet tops. They were sanded and shaped with rounded edges. It must have taken four men to carry those cabinet tops into their final resting place.

Stillwater sent us another group of men, and they made us filtering troughs for the cistern. They spent days putting guttering on the whole house and running that round pipe. They showed us how to waste the first few minutes of rain to wash the sand and grit off the roof then turn that diverter just so and they said it would fill the cistern. Wouldn't you know it, *no rain!* Sam said that the first time the cistern was filled it would taste like plaster. It didn't matter to me; I was ready for rainwater.

As soon as the wall plaster cured, the painters came back and decorated all the ceilings, walls, and woodwork to my wants. I had never made so many choices in my life, but we got the work done. Alex told me to go stay in the barn-house until the house was completed.

I thought, *Well! the ole bossy thing!* I could see the men cleaning up the kitchen area. The cistern was completed, the painting all done. The yard was raked, and then another wagon came in from Stillwater. More boxes, crates, and hammering. I flittered around and the morning came to unveil the new house. Alex came and took all the boys and me up to the back door. He stopped and thanked the Lord for the opportunity to build a new house and asked his blessing on all who trod these floors. We crossed ourselves as we began our journey into a new home.

The house showed us the fruit of all the laborers: a porch big enough to seat the grownups; I walked into the kitchen to a brand new wood-burning cookstove with hot water boiler on the side; I whirled around, and Alex was doing his smiling thing and said, "Now, now, Josie, we only get a new house once in this lifetime. Besides that, Joseph and Annie need the old one!"

The finish carpenters had made us a harvest table to seat twelve with leaves to seat more. The boys ran upstairs and started claiming the bedrooms for themselves, while Alex and I rambled through our master bedroom on the main floor. Our parlor could hold a whole batch of people! Our house had two chimneys, one for the cookstove and one for a very large pot belly stove, screens on all the windows, and not a shade tree close enough for shade.

As the boys filed back outside, all the talk was who could climb the stairs the fastest. I stopped those ruffians and laid down the law: no running on the stairs. They all muttered to themselves, "Yeah right!"

We spent the first night awake as owls, we couldn't get used to the new smells. I wanted to go get my horse just so I could smell him! We got those new smells covered over the first time I burnt the bacon, spilled a cobbler in a hot oven, and baked twelve loaves of bread. I think the worst thing that came in was my yellow cat that meowed around my feet. The first winter was cold, and my tomcat liked to get close to the wood cook stove to get warm. I had gotten up early that morning and built a good fire in the stove. I was mixing biscuit dough when I began to smell scorched cat. I jerked the door almost off its hinges, and a ball of yellow fur came out in a blur. I didn't have time to open the screen door because he went right through the center of the wire, squalling like a hot cat can. Alex came out of the bedroom and said, "Josie, you've burnt the, the—"

"Alex, don't you say a word; you go find my cat and see what you can do for the blisters that are on his feet!"

Alex came back in with a smile on his face and said, "Ole Yeller is kind of a burnt orange now with no whiskers. We won't have to worry about him getting into a warm oven anymore."

My cat came back the next morning and walked way around the stove; I guessed you could call him a suspicious, crispy critter.

I began to have those old tired, full feelings again, especially in the mornings. Childbearing was not done yet! My days of morning sickness would upset Old Bob, and he would come stand beside me till the urge was over for the day. I tried to ride him, but that time was over. Anne and Sara came regular and helped me with the housework and to catch up on the gossip. The new house was a marvel of invention; to have cistern water just outside the door was the best. Anne would bake bread twice a week, and I had to stay outside during the baking. I couldn't stand the smell of fresh bread! Sara said I had several weeks to go and went on home.

All the menfolk were gone to the fields. Annie was to come the next morning when my water broke. I'd been there before; there was no reason to get excited. I delivered Lambert before noon and fed that squalling boy all the milk he could nurse. I felt good enough to bake biscuits for dinner along with the soup of the day. The boys came in hungry as hounds and never noticed I had a slimmer build. Lambert squalled his best and woke my family from their doldrums.

"Mommy's had a baby!"

I nursed him again right in front of my family, and guess what? They did the dishes! Alex was so excited about going to get Sara. I shooed him out of my kitchen and said that I could manage. I rested the next day, and my men folk did all the chores. I though, *I can't live like this,* and started right in being the cook. Annie came to bake bread a day late and got so excited she forgot to put in the sourdough starter. I think the hogs liked the new feed: flat bread!

Homes were being built on each homestead when they had the materials and money. I asked Alex how we were getting along, and all I could get out of that German was a big *humph!* Alex had a constant stream of mares coming to his white donkey stud. I didn't get into his affairs, but he was constantly training and selling white mules that were ready to work.

Company Moving On

Sam and Nella had stayed on the farm for a while after the house was finished. I could see they wanted a place of their own, and they moved over to the sawmill area and share cropped with Ole. We visited back and forth some, and then Sam went to work for Ole full time. Nella helped Sara till one day Sam and Nella went back to Braymer, Missouri. We never heard from them again I missed their good humor and praised the Lord for the times we had together.

Alex and Lin went to a horse and mule sale in Yale one day and brought home a pair of oxen. I looked that bull over, and all I could see was a ton of meat. The cow was a mite smaller but the same color. I started to ask what we were going to do with oxen, but I held my tongue and got a right smart look see what an ox could pull. Alex wanted to clear more land, and that pair knew just what to do. I had heard that they could really pull, but to see them in action was a treat. The yoke went on them first, with just a small rope snapped into a nose ring. A large chain was strung between the oxen and through the yoke. Alex got his pair out and practiced with a sled. *Gee* and *haw* were all he spoke then stopped them with a tug on the nose ring. He gave the boys and me a ride around the barn so slow I could have walked faster than that!

The day came to start pulling stumps with the oxen; I was not going to miss this show. Alex got them in place, and one of the boys would hook the chain onto a medium-sized stump. All I heard was a *click click* coming from Alex, and things started happening. The oxen pulled up the slack and never stopped. Ever so slowly the stump gave up its grip in the ground. A small tug on the ring stopped the straining pair, and the first stump was lying out on its side. I thought, *this is too easy. What will happen with a big stump?* All this time the bull was chewing his cud with that "let's get on with the work sometime today" look!

We had a contest to name the oxen. I can't remember all the names, but Fred and Teddy seemed to fit. Alex trained the oxen to turn by their names instead of *gee* and *haw*. Their early training kept Fred on the left and Teddy on the right.

"*Fred,*" was drawn out and sure enough Fred pulled to the left. Teddy was spoken sharply and she pulled to the right.

I watched till I was tired and took my baby Lambert back to the shade. This went on for days, ever so slowly, till a ten-acre patch was cleared of all the unwanted stumps. The boys had teams of mules they used to pile up all the brush and stumps. All I had to do was to try to keep all those men full of food. Alex even trained the boys how to work those slowpokes. They said that drawn-out language that Fred and Teddy knew.

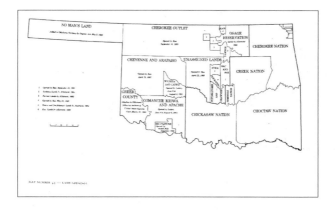

First Census

The day the twelfth census of the United States registered all of us in Eagle Township, Payne County, Oklahoma. A man by the name of Christian Wells wrote all our names in his book. I looked on and found most of our neighbors' names that had made the run in '93 were in the same book. We were officially in the census book! Census or no, we had to get back to work on our farm.

Fall

Alex kept the boys planting all our cleared land with corn, hay, oats, and more garden by the acre. We ran out of room in the root cellar and decided to enlarge the covered space. Alex hooked Fred and Teddy to the logs and piled them up with the stumps that were drying. He ran a cable around my drying shed and stacked it with the stumps. A good fire consumed the pile that was hot for days. They enlarged the root cellar with that same two-horse slip and put new logs on the top. This cellar had bins for the crops as they were harvested. The boys got so tired pulling the turnips, carrots, cabbage, potatoes, beets, crooked neck, and acorn squash; the very best keepers were pumpkins. That fall they said they never wanted to eat another veggie.

Of course, the carpenter, my Alex, built another smokehouse- drying shed that we could live in, it was so big. Ole had sawn some of the biggest timbers for the floor, and it all fit in like it had been made for the shed. I wondered then how long Alex and Ole had been planning on building a new smokehouse drying shed. The fruit trees were outstanding producers, and it took the whole family to store the fruit in the root cellar bins. Some time about then, Alex made me a drying rack out of tin. Positioned on the sunny side of the house, we would fill the trays and be able to dry six bushels at once. We dried peaches, apricots, all kinds of berries, pumpkin, and apple rings. Along after frost the boys would take all of us in the sled down to the Cimarron River to pick up pecans, walnuts, and hickory nuts. I would take a picnic basket to eat on the riverbank, and most of the time we shared our fare with some of the neighbors. We made friends with the Pawnees, Sac and Fox, Pottawattamie, and the Kanza tribes. The word was out that I was a healer, so I always took my tools of the trade to be a midwife. I didn't charge any money but was always rewarded with something.

A dear old soul came to call while down on the river bottom with the body rash; I helped her change clothes and saw the whip marks left over from the Indian repression. I couldn't find much wrong with her but the body lice that infected most camps. Some ground tea leaves and body powder relieved the itch, but the listening of her plight made her day. I took a mommy cat and four kittens as payment; I thought, *Oh well, I won't eat these cats, but we need more mousers to guard our farm.*

I found two black snakes one day and turned them loose in our root cellar. I should have told my boys to let them be. The first thing I knew that old Long Tom gun went off down in the cellar. I hurried out in time to see Lemoine coming out blinking like a pet coon; he couldn't hear a thing and the snake had gotten away. I was glad Alex had taught them not to use any shot. We would have lost a bushel of apples. Lemoine was trying to cry from having missed the snake. I gave him a cracker sandwich and thanked him for trying. He soon dried up, and I then told my menfolk not to bother my cellar snakes. My sweet Alex muttered something to the effect that if he found them out at the chicken house, he would cut their heads off with a double-bitted axe! I let well enough alone and told my snakes to stay in the cellar and catch all the mice and rats they wanted! My boys all shook their heads and said something about Momma talking to the animals again.

I wrapped an old broom with rags and put it at the door leading into the cellar. This batted the webs out of my way. I hated those spider webs hanging from the overhead logs. My family laughed to see my plight, but being a homesteader's wife you learn to cope with the insects. Flies were always a problem on the back porch; Alex solved that with hanging strips of rags over the doors and keeping them soaked with coal oil. I don't know if it killed any flies, but we didn't have any body lice to speak of.

BREAD DAY

Every three days, rain or shine, I had to bake bread, no matter who was visiting or working. I would catch at least three kids and spread out the table in the screened-in porch to mix twelves loaves of sourdough bread. Two big sifters of fresh ground wheat flour were put in each bread bowl, a handful of sugar, and I started them mixing with their hands. A double squint of salt with two hands full of hog lard in each bowl was mixed by hand with enough warm water to make pasty dough. Then we all got around and poured the two bowls out on my well-floured table. The fun part started then with the mixing in of three cups of sourdough starter. We would wear out just in time to let the dough sit for about one hour. I would hand-sift more flour into the next kneading. All this was done the night before and put into pans set up on the cook stove warmer. If we had a warm night, I would start baking bread before daylight in time for the hungry workers to have freshly baked bread for breakfast. If it was a cool night, my sourdough bread would have to be baked later in the day. Either way we had fresh baked bread for a meal. All my boys always had good timing coming in to eat that freshly baked bread.

Several dogs were kept to guard the farm, go hunting, or to tell us when we had company. The dogs hung around the back door to catch any leftovers. Therein lay the problem. I started noticing we were missing bread. Sometimes it had never been baked, and a whole loaf pan was left empty on the porch floor licked clean! I enjoyed a good mystery, and the next batch of bread was set out on the porch table to rise the first time. Wasn't long before a mother dog with pups scratched the screen door open and started in. I used my broom and sent them packing right back outside and kind of forgot the incident till the next time we baked bread. I heard all that growling and snapping of pups getting their fill of sourdough bread straight out of the bowl. I grabbed my broom and went at that litter—too late; the pups had chowed down half of my bread dough. They heard me coming and went through the screen with the door closed. It left me wondering what would happen to those pot-bellied pups! I thought, *Oh well, I don't want that dough now,* and moved the other bowl into the house. The boys came in and asked where the pups were. I shrugged my shoulders, Alex looked the other way, and we had dinner and still no pups at the back door. During my nap I was wakened by pups whimpering their heads off. I listened outside, and the sound was coming from under the porch floor. As the men folk came in for supper, they heard the racket and started trying to coach the pups out of the hole. My sourdough bread dough had started to rise in those paunches, and we had some very uncomfortable dog pups stuck under the porch! I acted dumb and told Alex the boys needed help calling the dogs. He promptly told me those boys could solve their own problems. Yes, a bigger hole was knocked in foundation. The pups got outside in time to lose their sourdough dinner, and Alex got to repair the foundation. Problem solved? Not yet. I got a new hook on the repaired screen door. The pups learned a lesson till the next baking bread time.

WILD GEESE

We lived within shouting distance of the Cimarron
River, and since sound travels both ways, we got to
hearing big gray geese one morning before daylight.
Honk-a-dee honk! Those old honkers were telling the
whole river bend that they were in from Canada. Alex
got the boys up early and loaded up a couple blunder-
bust shotguns with bird shot. I needed a good mess of
goose grease, the boys wanted to go hunting, and we
could just taste goose for dinner. I stayed at home to
get the pot a boilin' and heard the guns go off right
at daylight. I waited for the huntin' party to show up
and heard their banter from over yon hill. I had all the
spices laid out and saw they had gotten a skinny, tall
grey one. Those boys were proud as peacocks when in
they rode. I looked the bird over, picked up my spice
rack, and went back into the house. Alex told the boys
to pick the feathers clean and start boiling that bird
for dinner. Alex came into the house about to explode

laughing. The boys had killed a gray bird okay, but it was a crane about four feet tall.

"Alex, them boys—"

"Wait now, Josie. This can be a good lesson for those boys. They heard geese and shot that ole gray crane wishin' it was the same thing. Let's leave them alone to kill, clean, cook, and eat their catch."

I thought about the lesson to be learned and took my sweet boys the salt. They had gotten most of the wing feathers off when they discovered there wasn't much bird between the beak and the tail. Not to discourage their efforts, I suggested they just skin the crane and forget about all the tough feathers. With renewed effort, this did seem to work much better. I had the big iron pot boiling outside, and they deposited this sparrow-size bird in the water and started in cooking their dinner. So help me I could hardly keep from smiling. I went back inside and cooked Alex and me a good breakfast and left the chefs to their labors. The cooking spree took all day long, with me supplying their every need. Some time after dinner they pronounced the bird done. They came in sat the table, took a platter, and brought the specimen to be carved up. Alex and I said we weren't hungry and turned the feast over to the party.

Now this is what we heard; the spokesman said grace and the rest passed the plates to get their share. The old grey crane had turned into a knot of bones about the size of a cat's hairball; the number one chef hacked the carcass into chunks and divided the spoil. *Chomp, grind,* but no *slurp.* We heard the chairs scrape back from the table and en masse those boys exited the back door. End of story. Not quite ... Alex proclaimed that the dishes needed to be washed. For some reason the boys weren't hungry until suppertime.

Losin' Old Bob

We kept improving the farm and had fenced the entire quarter section to keep our stock in. They say fences make good neighbors; we had the best you could ever want across the trail intersection. Their names were William and Lousia Stoops. They were just like us. Several of their kids were born before coming into Indian Territory. A hill dugout housed all their family: dirt farmers trying to exist on those ole sandhill farms. As the years went by, we celebrated all the fourths of Julys, Christmas, and whatever birthdays needed a cake and singing together.

Louisa Stoops and I needed to go to Yale for supplies, so it was Old Bob's turn to pull a wagon. I knew it was too much for the old boy, but we weren't in any hurry. We started out early one morning and visited up a storm until a rain caught us just before getting to the Yale Trading Post. Sam May came out and said, "You women are sure brave getting out in weather like this."

I told that young whipper-snapper that we needed supplies, weather or no. Louisa and I kept up our chatter until finally Sam asked if there was anything else. We added a thing or two and said we wanted to get back before dark; right then Dahl came out and said, "The weather sure looks bad. You women better stay the night and get home in the morning." We treated him the same as Sam and got on the way.

As we got into our wagon, I could see Old Bob sure had his work cut out for him. The wagon was rounded up with a tarp tied down tight. We set out for home, and the skies opened up like somebody had sliced the bottom of the clouds. Louisa and I got drenched to the skin. My Old Bob did all right until we got to Big Creek and he would not go across. I was ready to take a strap to his hide when we saw a big tree float by! Louisa and I knew we were in for a long night, but we were committed out on the trail for home. We pulled the cover loose and got in out of the driving rain; that was all we could do. I don't know when the rain stopped, but we could hear Big Creek roaring. We slept some until I felt the wagon starting to move, and Old Bob went through the waters and made for home.

William Stoops was out looking for us on the road when we got to their house. He said that Alex and the boys were on the other side and for me to stay until the big draw went down on the road to our house. Louisa gave me a change of clothes, and we went to bed for the morning. William took care of Old Bob. Alex came before dark the next day and said we would have to go back to Big Creek and come in another way. I said I would harness Old Bob up and follow him.

"No, sweet Josie, Old Bob has pulled his last wagon."

"No, Alex, he is just asleep and I can wake him." I went out to the horse shed, and there stood my Old Bob with his head hanging down to the floor. He had pulled me the last time, and I never knew he was ailing! Alex had brought an extra set of mules and towed me and the wagon home. I told William not to bother Old Bob, and I would come back with a flat sled and haul him home. We went back to Big Creek; there was a ditch six feet deep that my Old Bob had crossed with his precious cargo. The wagon and his tracks were on each side of the creek but nothing between.

How did he get across? I pondered.

We took the flat sled back to the Stoops and loaded my steed ever so gently. We took him to the highest hill we had, laid him out like he was asleep, and gave him an Indian burial. I said to myself, *There lies a good old partner.*

I missed the intrusion of that plug around the farm and had to rely on the dogs to tell me if somebody was coming. Alex ever so gently offered any horse or mule on the farm to take his place.

"Not now, Alex. I just can't."

Little Elf came the next day to visit and water her horse. Tiny One was growing with leaps and bounds was sure a lap full. I took Little Elf up close to where I had laid Old Bob out the last time. As we drew closer, we could see plenty of the big circling birds and we didn't bother their task. Little Elf said she would come help me in time, and we would gather the bones and bury what was left.

"Thank you, Little Elf. I appreciate that."

Vision Quest

I heard the dogs announce we had company, and lo and behold in came Little Elf looking wild with tears in her eyes.

"Grandma Josie, can I borrow a coal oil lantern?"

"Why sure, child. Do you need extra oil?"

"Yes, Grandma, and can you keep Tiny One for a while I need to go visit the elders? I can't get Tiny One in the chambers."

I right quick shut my mouth. This small Indian was going on a Vision Quest, and I didn't have any business asking questions. Little Elf left her pony and just walked out of sight carrying the lantern. All my boys were so glad when they found Tiny One in the house; they soon learned that she was speaking two languages and starting to sign. Tiny One spoke with such a lilt we hung on every word. Alex and the boys asked where Little Elf was. I tried to describe an Indian journey of the mind, I think that was all they understood, and

Little Elf was visiting her elders. I didn't tell them her elders were all dead, and she was going to talk to them. I questioned myself about where she was going. All I could think of was she was going toward the Cimarron River bluffs.

Little Elf came back the next night, and the dogs heralded her to the barn. I took her some jerky and coffee and found a sleeping Little Elf all scratched up. I left the jerky but wondered how she had scratched her head so. She came up from the barn for dinner the next day much revived. I asked about the lantern, and all she would say was, "I couldn't get it out of the chamber. Grandma Josie, I've had the most refreshing vision, and I'm going to step over the bow with a brave when I get back to the camp. Will you clean up my head so it won't show so much?"

Again I didn't ask any questions, as a good head washing got most of the dried blood out. Some soothing suave put a smile on her face, and they left on her pony. One thing you learn is not to ask questions around the Indians; if they want you to know something, they will tell you in time.

Little Elf came back in a couple months all smiles.

"Oh, Grandma Josie, my new brave is so nice. Thank you for keeping Tiny One, she has filled our ears with newly learned names of your boys. Grandma Josie, can you go with me over to the river bluffs? Your lantern is still over in the chambers, and I need to show you my sign. Oh, and we will need to take more oil to see inside."

"Why, yes, Little Elf. Let's take something to eat and stay the day."

"Okay, but you will need to wear some old clothes."

I rattled around in the back of our closet and came out with an old pair of Alex's pants and shirt and thought, *I wouldn't just do this for any body*—the idea, me wearing men's clothes. Old shoes of Lin's put us on the trail to Big Spring. I thought, *I bet we're the first people to walk this way in decades.*

Little Elf and Tiny One were setting the fast pace, and I soon tired and asked for a stop.

"Little Elf, why are we going so fast? Where are you taking me?"

"Oh, Grandma Josie, I'm sorry. I forget that you're getting old!"

Humph! I did ask for that one.

"Little Elf, if I'm old enough for you to call me grandmother, then slow down and tell me where we're going."

The impish grin told volumes. "Grandma, you are the first one to know that I'm going to have another child, and I want you to see where I first knew it.

"Grandma, we are going to start at the halfway point of the Pawnee Trail called Big Spring. This spring has been used by the Indian Tribes since the river began running. This land belongs to you now, and we want to have a powwow on your land."

I had a hard time catching up with the talk, and then it hit me: *Little Elf is asking me to use our land.*

"Why, land sakes yes, Little Elf, but the river is another half mile east.

"No, no, Grandma Josie, this spring is part of the Cimarron River, and it runs way up on your land."

I was getting a geography lesson and couldn't believe it.

"Little Elf, how do you know its part of the Cimarron River?"

"Oh, Grandma, it's written in the chambers by the ancients of old. I don't even know how long it's been there, but we can count if we have enough lamp oil."

Little Elf sure had my attention. We got back on the Pawnee Trail.

"Little Elf, can you prove that this trail has been here for a long time?"

"Oh sure, Grandma, when we get close to the river, let's be on the lookout for a cut in the red sandstone."

Little Elf sat a leisurely pace, and I began to get my Indian breath back. Little Elf and Tiny One ran ahead and urged me on to a cut in the sandstone rock overlooking the Cimarron River. I looked this over and couldn't tell one rock from another. Little Elf kept up her pace until the red sandstone showed deep grooves. I couldn't believe my eyes; deep grooves made from centuries of traverse poles being dragged by the squaws. I could just imagine the sights along the Pawnee Trail, then seeing the halfway point to the "winter over" camps of the tribes. I let my imagination run on ahead, no, back in time before the horses came about four hundred years ago. Ole Coronado couldn't have imagined the prize he gave to the Indians when he turned them loose. They multiplied and made the best ponies ever born. Visions of Ole Bob came flooding back. I had to sit down and have a good cry. Little Elf came and stood by me, never saying a word. Tiny One sat on my lap, and I thought, *To have friends that are quiet is priceless.* I had thought I was over Old Bob, but he was still there strong as ever. He had carried me when I was down, I had nursed him back to life when he didn't care; I guessed we were even.

Little Elf started back in with the telling that this

was what the ancients called Vision Bend on the Pawnee Trail.

"In the cool of the evening, when the sun shines on the east bluff, they told of countless victories. Every tribe member could sit on the west side of the river and watch the bluff on the other side shine its colors. Vision Bend was the favorite place to take a nap, play in the water, or the water always furnished fish by the tote full. Buffalo roamed the 'winter over' sites, countless in number. Elk, deer, a stinky little pig could always be found. Grandma Josie, those times are gone now. There are way too many people for any game to grow. The white people seem to know how to grow animals, plant gardens, farm the land, live in houses, but the Indians won't let go of the past. I've come to Vision Bend and always got the same vision: Step across the bow, take your man, and go live like the white men, raise animals, plant crops and live in a house."

"Yes, Little Elf, that is exactly what I have done. It's hard changing your life to live like someone else, but it's the only thing to do now. Little Elf, I'm tired out today. Let's go see those chambers another day. I need to get back to the farm and fix supper; you need to go feed your man and the child inside of you. Another time will show itself to see your tribe's history."

We parted company for the time being, and I made the mental note to hear Little Elf out. I walked right back by Big Spring, and its being took on all new meaning for this half-Indian woman. Yes, Little Elf came back in a few days just full of news.

"Another old brave was up on his final resting place. Tiny One had learned to speak both languages like a Magpie and was practicing sign language with me."

Little Elf and I made plans to take a wagon and

camp out on Vision Bend until we were satisfied. We were going to make that plan come true as our crops were the bin. We even had help from Little Elf's husband, Joe. They came over to learn how to farm. We needed the help, and I had more mouths to feed and the very best friend to talk woman talk with. Our plans were sealed with the menfolk promising to clean the house once a day whether it needed it or not. My boys promised to make Tiny One teach them how to say their names in Cherokee, then the very best to take her swimming in the spring each day. Those dark eyes and smile always made our day.

Our wagon trip to Vision Bend was way too short. We didn't have time to talk ourselves out. The weather couldn't have been better as we camped on the east of the Cimarron River so I could walk to the chambers of old. Little Elf strung a rope down to the entrance for me to cripple along. I should have known she could run all the way inside. My first trip was a step back in time of Indian lore of the ancients. Painted just inside on a huge rock was a sign of the great spirit of the Osages, "Wah Kon Tah"; another sigh was of the calumet or sacred smoking pipe. As Little Elf led me in, she lit the ceremony pipe, and we both had to take a few puffs. I about gagged but held my peace until she turned the other way, *spitooee!* I could just imagine the countless lips that had caressed its stem and said those holy words of their religion just to please the gods. Enough was enough as we wriggled ourselves in the inner chamber.

The sun was shining through the long slit, and I was amazed at the amount of pictorials on the stones. I asked Little Elf, "How many years have the Indians drawn on the rocks?" She followed the thought with, "Grandma Josie, there is no end or start of these pictures. We are in the first chamber, and I was in the ninth when I ran out of oil in the lantern. I had to leave the lantern there and stumble my way out of the chambers to your house. That's when I about busted my head open on the sides of the rooms."

"Little Elf, I've had all the close places that I can stand for one day. Let's go camp for the night and start back in the morning."

"No, Grandma, we can't come into the chambers in the morning. You can't see anything but the fog!"

I had to get back outside so I could get my breath. In my hurry I banged my head on the Great Spirit rock and thought I was gone. I woke to Little Elf wiping my brow with a wet rag; I tried to sit up and swooned again. Some time in the night the world stopped whirling around, and I got so I could sit up.

Humph! This is crazy, Josie. Get more sleep and by morning you can stand up.

Little Elf was right; by morning the fog was pouring out of the chambers so thick it looked like smoke. I must have needed more sleep, as it was dinnertime before hunger woke me again, and there was Little Elf singing her crooning sounds. I was fully awake for dinner but the thoughts of going back into the belly of the earth put me back on my pallet. I thought I heard someone calling my name and passed it off until I heard it again.

"*Grandma Josie,* come help me," was what I heard from my mind fog.

I finally roused enough to realize it was Little Elf in the chambers. I very carefully held to the rope and just couldn't make myself go into the darkness. I answered, and almost immediately Little Elf spoke out loud, "Grandma Josie, I'm stuck in between two rocks and can't pull my foot out."

"Little Elf. take your moccasin off and spit on your ankle. Sometimes that will help."

Silence, then a low, soft rumble.

"Little Elf, are you okay?"

Silence.

"Grandma Josie, I think that last rumble let me free, but my ankle is broken. I can't see, make some noise."

So help me all that I could think of was to croon some nameless tune. Oh well, noise is noise. I can't say how long I crooned, but I couldn't make spit on the ground when Little Elf crawled out of the entrance. She collapsed in my arms, and I knew right then we were in for a hard time. Her leg was broken just below the knee. As she was passed out, I straightened it out and wrapped my bonnet around the calf really tight. Took the strings and knotted them around and around those staves. A soft moan came from the small woman, and I thought, *This is going to be hard getting her into the wagon and back to the house.*

Little Elf came around and said her leg felt better and we best be getting home as fast as possible, for the river was going to come up real fast. What a thing to think of now that child is babbling! We three-legged up to the wagon and got her over the backboard when she collapsed again. I slam-banged our camp gear into the wagon and hitched the horse and down to the river we flew. As the horse stepped into the calm water, I could hear the roar of million of tons of water coming at breakneck speed. I used the lines on that horses hide, and she stepped right across the waters. I look back now and I'm sure she walked on water. Either way we had to keep moving, for the water was coming up

PAT LORETT

so fast. We made it up to the cut in the west bank in time to see another million trees riding the crest of the wave. I shuddered to think what would have happened if we had been caught in that torrent. Just then I saw several head of dead cattle that had been caught out in the river; my question was answered.

Little Elf came to as I pulled up to the spring. We watched until Little Elf spoke rather loudly, "Grandma Josie, this is not the spring we need to watch; it's the one closer to your barn!"

We circled by our house and got all the menfolk we could and told them to move the stock out of the way of the spring up on our hill. Alex, always the calm one, spoke with his drawl, "Josie, we don't have a spring up on yon hill."

Little Elf blurted out, "Oh, Alex, you will have. The river is out of its banks and will come up even more. Come go with us and we'll show you what we mean."

I drove to another rock outcropping, and before we got there we could hear the rising waters coming. Alex shouted down the hill to the boys and told them to lead all the stock to higher ground. The first gush was clear and cool, but the next was Cimarron Red water. It gushed and spread out under the barn and corral then slowly went over the top rails and stayed there.

We took Little Elf to our house where I set the leg again and bound it up with tree bark and strips of rags. This brought on the telling of the Pawnee Trail with the chambers of information written by no telling how many people.

"Little Elf, how did you know the river was coming up?"

"Josie, you remember the fog we saw this morning and how strong it was coming up?"

"Yes, what made it do that?"

"Oh, Grandma Josie, I just couldn't leave your lantern back in those ole chambers, so I went back inside with more oil and got your lantern going and was reading the history of the chambers. I found your farm, Big Spring, and the other spring that is up on your hill. We must have had an earthquake from all the rumbling, and I got scared and tried to run out with your lantern. I fell down; the lantern went out; the rocks slipped and caught my leg. I hollered, cried, spoke to my god, spoke to your God, nothing helped until you came to the entrance and ordered the rock to move."

"Oh, Little Elf, don't tell falsehoods. I can't make rocks move. I told you to take your moccasin off and spit on your ankle. Sometimes that will help."

"Now, Grandma Josie, I heard you talking to God, and maybe he answered your prayer and moved the rock."

The Cimarron River came up overnight and went down overnight; the springs all got a good cleaning out. The horse corral dried up in a couple of days, and they let the horses and mules back in. The very first thing they did was have a good roll in all that mud. Made Alex mad, he just left them dirty. Alex made Little Elf a crutch and sent her and the gabby Tiny One home. They came back in time and said we should all go over and see the chambers, I told that crippled girl, "No, no, not again. That river can take care of itself."

"Grandma Josie, come take us over there in your wagon and we'll all take a look." We hitched the sled behind some green, broke mules and had the ride of our lifetime. As we neared the cut in the west bank, we soon realized the river had taken the whole west side down the river and ground it up to sand. East side?

PAT LORETT

A mess of tangled rocks with not a hint of what had been there. We looked at each other and shrugged our shoulders. There wouldn't be anybody who'd believe us if we were to tell it one hundred years from now ... or would they?

Naming the Last

The next morning I knew I was going to have another boy. Lambert was three years old; it was about time to add to the family. Waves of morning sickness flooded my body. For the next six weeks every morning those waves demanded my attention. I wondered what was different as weight came on like spring rains.

"Alex, I need to go see Sara. Something is wrong, and I can't seem to quit the morning sickness."

"Yes, Josie, we'll do just that. I can see you struggling."

A young set of white mules took us over to Sara's house, and wouldn't you know it, those queasy feelings left me as soon as they came in the middle of the river! I felt fine and wanted to go back home as we arrived at the sawmill, a very quiet sawmill.

"Alex, there is nobody home. Where is Sara's donkey? Why isn't the sawmill running? Where is everybody?"

"Josie, stop all the questions. I don't know anymore than you do."

Alex found a cold boiler, no mill hands, and about then we began to hear Sara's donkey up on the hill. We hurried ourselves around the spring and met Ole and Sara coming down the hill at that donkey's slow walk. Sara and I ran to each other and couldn't talk fast enough; all we could do was hug each other over and over. Those two had taken a wedding anniversary trip and wound up farther than they expected. We came along and found that giggling pair coming in from an all-night fling. We chastized them with, "We thought you two were too old for that sort of thing."

They blushed their best and Ole came back with, "You two don't know everything!"

"Josie, you're going to have another child soon!"

"No, Sara, I've got several months to go yet."

"Now, Josie, you can't fool me. I've seen this too many times. You are going to deliver in the next two months."

I told her about my morning sickness stopping as soon as we crossed the river, how I had been so sick.

"Josie, come into the house and let the menfolk talk outside. We'll figure this out."

Out came a listening horn, and I let Sara listen to my swollen middle. I couldn't tell anything until her expression changed to one of wonder.

"Josie, let's have a morning cup of coffee and we'll talk this out."

I thought, *What can happen now?*

"Josie, I want to take back what I said about you having a child in two months. I agree with you, that child will not be here for several months. This time you will have to go to bed and stay there. I will stay with you and we will need all the help we can get."

"Aw shaw, Sara. I have had six boys already and I feel fine. What can be worse than that?"

"Josie, I'm not trying to scare you, but you are going to have the biggest child yet!"

We seemed to run down with all this news, and I grew tired so fast.

"Josie, let me fix you some of my strong tea and you go take a nap."

It didn't take me long to agree to that. My tea and her crooning did its trick and I slumbered the afternoon away.

"Alex and Ole, come back to the park area. I want to talk to you." Sara told them all that she knew, and a plan was formed to take me back home and what to expect the coming months.

We made the trip back across the Cimarron River to our home and began the summer planning. Alex got the boys together, and we formed a plan for the coming boy. I tried to keep the house, but nothing seemed to work for long. Sometimes all I could do was sit in my rocker and cry. Alex would come in from the field work and nothing was fixed for supper. I felt so depressed that nothing was getting done, I would cry some more. Alex said he was going to the mill and would be back the next day. I flew mad and threw my beads at him going out the door. I had feelings of wanting to go back to Braymer, Missouri, not having this baby; Alex came back in time to catch me as I fainted.

I awoke that evening somewhat refreshed with Sara standing over me with her hands on her hips.

"Well, well, young lady, I see you have been trying to do too much and didn't send for me!"

I tried to retort something and busted out crying, followed by a cistern of tears.

"Oh, Sara, I can't seem to get anything done. This kid is about to tip me over forward, the days are too hot, the nights I freeze to death, and Alex doesn't know what to do!"

"Yep, that's the way it's going to be, but we will get through this birthin'," Sara came back.

Sara called Alex and the boys in to have a family planning. Sara explained what it was going to take to get through the next month.

"Josie is to stay in bed! I'm going call in Annie, Little Elf, and anybody else who will help. Annie said that she would make all the bread. The boys are to clean the house once a week whether it is needed it or not."

Sara was to come when she could, and she would be here for the next boy. This set the whole family into action, and I got back to be normal again. I found out if I asked real nice they would do or get anything I wanted. I got back to doing tatting again; my hands were so stiff from doing housework that they hurt along with my body. As my time drew near, Alex moved another bed in my bedroom. Sara and I got caught up with our gossiping ... yes, I said gossiping. We declared a time set aside to talk about anybody or anything, and I grew to the size of an elephant.

By this time we had a doctor in Yale, and he came out and told Sara and me that it was going to be the biggest baby he had ever delivered. I smelled his whisky breath and about ran him off right there. Sara gave me that "be quiet" look, and I held my tongue. We talked together and figured out the ole sawbones was looking for money, well, good riddance.

Little Elf came with the soup of the day several

times a week. Annie was baking the best bread by this time that she called her "hot stuff." I couldn't figure out what it was till one day I saw her mix red hot pepper in the pasty dough. My menfolk would sop up any leftover gravy with her bread and smack their lips. Food took on a greasy, slick taste, and Sara knew my time was close. I went into labor one afternoon, and Alex sent for the doctor. I was so sick; I just wanted it all to be over. My pains got closer and harder as the darkness closed in around the farm and still no doctor. Sara delivered me a half-grown boy that night. The doctor came the next day and said the boy weighed thirteen and a half pounds. Checked us over and said something about how frontier women don't need much help. I told Alex to give him a jar of my moonshine and send him on the way to Yale. We didn't hear any more from the doctor after that, except that he had arrived in town drunk as a skunk and was trying to tell about the twenty-pound boy he had delivered out by the Cimarron River. We didn't tell anybody where he had been, and he never remembered that all he did was weigh my baby that night.

I didn't recover very quickly from childbirth this time, and Sara pronounced, "Josie, this is the last child you will bear."

I was devastated as Sara went on.

"Now, Josie, there are not many women who will carry seven straight boys to manhood. Let's praise the Lord for what you have and get ready for a whole string of grands!"

Hmm, the very thought of grandchildren did have a good ring to it.

As Baby grew we had the dilemma of naming our last boy. I had run the complete list of L's and nothing connected; for the time being we settled on Baby. We were so busy that three years slipped by. He was almost three years old and was not weaned as of yet when it hit me that boy was too big for me to nurse! We had company, and here came Baby pawing me like some pig, you know *grunt, squeal*... the very idea. I moved his bed upstairs, put up a fence on the stairway, and let him cry. I don't know who suffered the most, my family or Baby. That was the final straw; he cried for nights on end till I got my fill of his squalling. A peach switch put that boy back in his own bed. Then and only then could Alex and I rest all night long. I was not mean to John Clifford Lorett, but I had babied him much too long. He grew six inches the next year on solid food.

Good Times, Bad Times

I can't remember what year it was when we got our first mowing machine that was pulled by a team of mules. Alex was so proud of it that he taught the bigger boys how to use it. I called it our *click-a-tee;* it made the most pleasing sound cutting the hay in swathes. Our stationary bailer would be set up out in the fields. Alex trained his white donkey to supply the power round and round. As I remember, it took our whole family to put up hay. Mowing, raking, bucking, bailing, and then the whole family would gang up, haul those bales, and store them in our hayloft. Seems to me we baled hay twice a year. I had to fix a string of meals each year just for haying. Our mule crop each year helped pay the operation of the farm and then the crops paid the rest.

We sold beef to the Yale Trading Post until oil was discovered on the other side of the river. There were so many people living in Oilton, Drumright, and Silverton, I think they slept with their feet in each other's

PAT LORETT

tents. We got to taking farm produce to the oil patches
and would sell out ever time we went. We had an apple
tree that never produced an apple of any size. Didn't
make any difference; those knotty things went east and
were given away as soon as we opened up for business
out of the back of a wagon.

Alex sometimes had a cow or a bull that wouldn't
breed. As soon as they fatted up, they would slaughter
them early one morning and lay the carcass in a wagon
box and head for the oil patches. I didn't ask many
questions, but they always took a sharp knife and axe
to cut the animals up. Alex said he could make more
selling meat to the oil patch people than to the butcher
shops. He would come back with a clean wagon box
from going through the river. They would be back
before noon looking for some other critter that looked
ailing. We never slaughtered any mules or horses, but I
bet they would have sold too.

Our boys loved to go to the oil patches and get
into the business of selling over the tailgate of the wagons. People would just beg for bread, and I found out
I couldn't supply enough to fill their needs. We had
seen hard times after the run of '93, but this was the
hardest of the good times. I didn't let on that I was a
midwife; they would have run me ragged. I was busy
enough fixing meals and taking care of my family that
I just couldn't help them much.

Losin'

I must tell you about Lemoine, and maybe my heart-ache will go away in time. The boys always played till they were bone tired and then they would do the evening chores. Lemoine came in one night saying his back hurt. I looked him over and put some salve on a cut. I found him in the night with a high fever, I did what I could do, and by morning I knew he was really sick. We took him to the doctor, and he found a weed had stuck in between two bones in his back. The doctor called Alex and me in his office and said the boy would not live the next night through. We took the boy home, and, sure enough, we had to have a funeral the next day. Alex built him a good stout box, and I laid him out in his best clothes. The community gathered abound the gravesite in Greenwood Cemetery and laid him to his final rest after dinner. Our first funeral in this new land about tore our hearts out. Alex made arrangements with the Greenwood trustees for twenty-four burial sites that day for any Lorett to have a final resting place. Alex and I stood around our newly acquired land that day and showed the boys where we were to be buried when our times came.

Grands

To have grandchildren was always a hope of mine, and I lived for the day when they would be under my feet. My first one was Leona, a fine blonde-haired scamp, I coddled on my lap. I know I won't get the eighteen in order, but here goes: Leona, Lucille, Bea, Willard, Aloysius, Leon, Joe, Jack, a stillborn girl, Sanford, Mary Jean, Tommy, Ruth, Robert, Donald, Clifford, Minnie, and my youngest, Pat. They came and went around my feet, much to my joy. I enjoyed their antics to the point I would get into the fray, then the real joy began. Alex would wrestle them to the ground, and in time they got him down too.

MY PET GOAT

We had one of those summers when everything grew like our boys were. The men folk had fenced me a small garden space for my herbs, and I hand-carried all my wash water to each hill. It sounds healthy, but that soon grew out of hand. I didn't want to do away with any of my precious plants, so Alex said, "Let's put a few goats in the fenced part and let them have a go at fresh herbs."

"Yes, that sounds like a good idea. In fact, get me some milk goats, and I'll make goat cheese at the same time."

I saw the wagonload of goats coming one day, and we had instant trimmers in the overgrown patch. The little kids played till they fell over in exhaustion. As we watched them, I noticed we had a small buck with horns just starting to grow. This became a huge problem!

Old Hornie, as we called him, took it upon himself

to butt my backside when I wasn't looking! I put up with this beast one butt too long, and he left black and blue strips the size of his horns in all the wrong places. My pan of water went up in the air, I fell down in the sage patch, my glasses got stuck up in a trumpet vine, and Old Hornie went looking for something else to butt. I got back on my feet and had to call one of the boys to find my glasses. As soon as I could see again the goat and I had a set to about his bad habit. By this time the menfolk had gathered outside the fence with their guns drawn, savoring the thought of roast goat for supper. I relented and said, "Don't you boys hurt my goat. We need his services once in a while, but while you're here, I want a large steel post set in the ground with twenty-four inches sticking out." I found my he-goat and started berating his bad habit as the post was set. The menfolk all went off after the post setting, mumbling something about Momma talking to the animals again!

I let the matter settle a few days and put my outside apron on backwards, took the back out of my bonnet, and put it on backwards also. I stepped astraddle of my post; this let me see the most educational animal behavior ever. I know this a stretch of my imagination, but my Hornie never knew the difference. I can see him now, getting all lined up with you-know-what. My apron was draped over the steel post. I was humming some nameless tune when his final charge put him in motion toward my back-front side. As his two horns connected with that steel post, I took my apron strings and tied the apron around and around that passed out he goat! I thought, *His limp body means we have roast goat!* Hornie finally came to a twitching and was able to stand but couldn't see anything but white. All he knew to do was back up, which he did all afternoon, especially while the boys were washing up for supper. They nudged each other and laughed off their backsides as Alex came in.

"Boys, don't say a word about this. Nobody will believe what goes on around the Lorett house."

My sweet Hornie finally wore the apron to a frazzle, and never did I have a problem with his horns again. All I had to do was flip a white cloth and he would shake his head, like he was saying, "No, no, no."

Feedin' the Preacher

Our neighbor about two sections away was a traveling preacher, the kind that worked like a slave all week then traveled anywhere to preach the gospel. It was not unusual for him to have a wedding before and after the services, preach a funeral at the graveside anytime, and then go home to work and have more kids. He brought ten kids with him and his sweet wife from Arkansas, and then they had six more after the land run of '93. Alex and I met them right after the run and found them to be the best of neighbors. We had a perfect brush arbor church around our big spring, with shade trees all over the hillside. The menfolk would meet before the camp meeting and build a brush arbor that would shade fifty or sixty people. All us women would plan meals around whatever the families would bring each evening. After supper the music would start and we sang all the ole timey songs that had been around forever. It wasn't impossible for us to have ten or twelve instruments and lots of specials.

Our neighbor preacher always called the ordained men forward to have a prayer meeting during the singing. The singing would finish up with "Rock of Ages" and "Sweet Hour of Prayer," just to get the preacher started.

W.H. Fritch would start in so quiet you had to lean forward to hear him. As he warmed up, you could sit back comfortable-like. Two hours later he would be completely wet from sweat, and you could hear him without any problem.

Sure as anything, as soon as the meeting would draw to a close he would ask if there was any food left. All sixteen of his children would be in line first, mixed in with our seven boys. We got used to this style of feeding our families and fed the preacher his due. We all went home filled with the spirit and praising the Lord for a close neighbor who could fill the pulpit. Our campground got the trees all grubbed out in the following years, and we sure liked the company.

My Horse Blackie

Another animal showed up one day, led to our farm by Alex himself, the most gallant black Morgan with all the shiny harness of the day. Just behind that black beauty was a covered surrey with zip insides. I had been busy kneading bread and I looked a mess, but it took my breath away.

"Oh, Alex, he's beautiful. Can I use him to go on call?"

"Sweet Josie, this horse is to be yours. He is green broke now, but you know horses and he will gentle down soon."

Alex put him in his own stall, and I got ready for the ride of the day. You should have seen him throw a fit at seeing a woman with an apron on.

"Hmm," said Alex. "Maybe we should let him settle some and start at daybreak."

I was disappointed at the setback but made the daylight come alive with my crooning. I had dressed in black, just like my horse. He was an altogether different animal. I took him out to a strong post set in the ground and put the saddle and bridle on that green broke horse. I thought he would break his neck. He and I had an understanding that morning as to who was boss. By noon he had relented to letting me stand beside his withers and pet him with a curry comb. By mid-afternoon he really wanted water, and he let me lead him around the corral stopping by the water trough. Each time he would relent I would curry his black hide. By mid-afternoon we really were getting tired, and I could step up in the stirrups. I took the tack off and on him several times, and I knew we were going to get along fine. I fed and watered him over the progression of several days as Blackie became my horse.

He gentled right down, and I started in with the surrey. He got used to that again, and I got my first ride in time and planned out how I could train him to go home. We had an old mare that I had named after my friend Nelle that would go home from anywhere in the river bend area. I took her along on night rides and would turn the reins loose, and, of course, Nelle trained Blackie to go right back home.

In time my horse took me on the rounds of midwifery of the community. I was known in all the River Bend area as Grannie Josie, and everybody looked out for me.

FLU 1918–1920

I feel I must take time to tell you in-depth about the flu epidemic during and after the First World War. War broke out in some nondescript town in Europe and spread like wildfire. The first we heard was a clarion call for men to join the army and fight Germany. Some of our boys were the right age to join, and they talked at length when to go. As it turned out, some of them were already married with families. Most were too young, and all were farmers who were desperately needed to raise food. We buckled down and planted the maximum acres of feed grains, took care of what we had, and served our country right there in Payne County, Oklahoma. We did not make excuses; we all worked like slaves for the good of the United States of America.

Enough talking about the war across the waters. We had just as much of a war right here. We never knew who brought the Spanish flu home with them, but come back it did. The first I knew of it was over on the Cimarron side of our place. A small girl came one morning looking for Grannie Josie. I stepped outside just in time to see the girl pass out on my own back step. Always one to be cautious about the plague, I looked the girl over and discovered her high fever. I pulled my family back and told them not to get close to her. I put the girl in my surrey, and Blackie took me to her family. I found the whole family sick with high fever, coughing, and wheezing; all this meant one thing, a plague of colds was going through the river bend, and I best find out what was being spread around. While I was trying to make the lot feel better, I discovered a soldier boy back from the war in the barn. He was so sick his eyes were turned up over the top of his head. What I could see and hear was the family was sick; this scared me. I backed out into the open and pondered what I could do.

First things first, I took a white sheet and stretched across the front gate to keep people out. I sent my Blackie home with a note to bring me food and water for several days and to go get the doctor, for I thought we had a case of the plague and for him to stay on the outside of the sheet. I didn't have to wait too long before my family brought my things and said a boy had gone to Yale to find the doctor. I gave all the family some cough syrup to make them sleep, started to cook some soup, and heard the doctor coming on a run. I ran out to the sheet and the doctor was there with quarantine signs, nailing them on a post. *Keep out!*

I recognized my drunken friend, but he was all business by this time.

"Grannie Josie, have you been around the sick folks?"

"Doc, a very sick girl came to my house and passed out on my back stoop. I kept my family back and hauled her home and found the whole clan sick abed. Doc, I'm scared that this might get out in the whole countryside. What can we do?"

"Grannie Josie, I don't have a cure for this Spanish flu. All the soldier boys who are coming back from the war seem to be carrying some bug with them. How do you feel?"

"Doc, I feel fine now, but I'm sure I've been exposed to whatever is being spread around."

"Okay, Grannie Josie, you stay away from anybody and treat the family the best you can. Don't you have some herb for the high temp?"

"Doc, I thought you didn't believe in herbs. What has gotten into you?"

"Grannie Josie, I got exposed about ten days ago, and I have began running a fever at night. I need to go to bed, but I'm sure we're in for a long siege of colds. I'm trying to stay away from people, but you know that is impossible for a doctor. Grannie, if you find out anything that will help, please let me know. Do you have any shine with you?"

I was right mad and accused the doctor of being a drunk.

"Yes, you are right, Grannie, but I'm running out of something to drink, and I need your help."

I had the top hand by then and took my advantage to the max.

"Doc, you don't need my help. You need to stop drinking so much."

"Okay, Grannie Josie, if you will help me, I will cut back from so much drinking."

"Nope, Doc, if you want my help, you have to quit cold turkey!"

All I heard was some muttering, and finally he agreed to stop when we got the flu under control. I thought, *Well, that old sawbones does have a heart after all.*

I had Alex bring me a fruit jar of shine over, and I started right in making cough syrup. I mixed eucalyptus, honey, pine tar, and shine and brought the entire pot to a boil to thicken up. I don't know what I did wrong, but nobody could have taken it. Now I was desperate. I could feel fever coming in on me, so I had Old Man Sigh come talk to me over the quarantine signs. I told him what I had done; he scratched his stubby jaw and nodded his all-knowing look. I thought, *I hope nobody finds me talking to the whisky peddler; my reputation will be tarnished for sure.* Sigh started right in explaining the process of making cough syrup.

"Josie, leave making shine with cough syrup ingredients to us that know how."

I told him to hurry and make me several bottles of the secret medicine and that I was getting sick myself. He came back the next morning with twelve bottles and said to give a small child a spoonful two times a day, two spoonfuls to a half-grown child, and a half cup to an adult.

I hurried him off and administered the medicine to each one of the sick family. I though I'd bypass the spoon and chug-a-lugged my own measure. I awoke hours later to the sound of children playing in the yard. Ma and Pa had covered me up on the front porch and let me snore to my heart's content. Our fever was down some, and I was weak as a cat. We got some soup down and all of us got our second dose after supper. I awoke in the night to the most awful snoring sounds of a resting family; this cure must have been all right, for we were still alive. I called for the doctor the next day and found out he was in bed in Yale, sick as a horse. I turned the family loose with another bottle of cough syrup with the instructions not to take too much. Blackie took me home, and my boys found me in my surrey covered up in a blanket snoring the next morning.

I came around and remembered that the doctor was sick in Yale. I took him a bottle of the cure, and he flat dab refused to take his dose. I had to tell him what the cure had done for me and the family that was so sick. He relented and gagged his half a cup down. Almost immediately he was asleep, and I left him in charge of a midwife. I had four bottles of medicinal cough syrup left. I went straight down to Sigh's place, and they wouldn't let me talk to him; said he was busy down on the river.

Yeah right, he's busy making moonshine I thought! I went on home and he got to my house as soon as I did.

"Oh, Josie, I'm glad you come to see me. I've made a mistake a making that cough syrup. It's twice as strong as it should be. I hope you haven't taken too much."

"Sigh, I don't want you to change the recipe one bit. In fact, I hope you have made more because it has already cured that family of the Spanish flu."

We sat out under the shade tree that day, and I ordered a continuous supply of the medicinal alcohol. Sigh told me to charge fifty cents a bottle for the cough syrup; I told him that I was not going to peddle moonshine for him! He settled for chicken at supper and went home full as a tick.

I made more calls to the families that had the Spanish flu, and the community never knew who supplied the cure. We lost two dozen people in the river bend to that plague, but none who took our cure were lost. Where the flu came from or where it went we never knew, but we won that war in our own territory. Doctor? Oh, he survived the flu and made good on his word about drinking too much. I never told where the cough syrup came from. I called him a quack and he called me a faith healer. Deep down inside we needed each other, and the community was all the better for us.

Mule Farm

My future-thinking Alex always dabbled in the mule business. His specialty was white, spotted, white stocking feet, mane and tail, then the last requirement, big! Some of his brood mares were draft horses with feet the size of dinner plates that stood eighteen hands or taller. Alex wanted a mule to weigh fifteen weights or more. His donkeys always had to be white and have a gentle disposition. Our pulling stock was widely known in Payne County. As soon as a foal was born, the boys started petting them when they nursed. The foals began to wear a halter and were tied up to begin their training. Of course, our mares were as gentle as pets can be, and this trained our mules to be the same. Once in a while we would get a young mule that wanted to bite. A good understanding about feed, water, and petting got them over that problem.

It seemed Alex had a knack for the equine as he spent countless days training young teams. His specialty was selling matched trained teams ready to work on the farms. One of his tricks was having them pull a two-wheeled cart around the farm in the soft sand. If anyone wanted a free ride, they were to just jump aboard and ride to their heart's content or their backside was tired. Every team had to go through the thought of running away. "No problem," said Alex. "I help them run faster."

My kind, gentle Alex was never one to beat an animal, but his black snake snapped over the long ears of a mule would get you a fast ride around the whole farm in the soft sand. Those green broke mules would just think they were going to get a good strapping, but a good run around a section would tire the best. That black snake would get you another trip. The next round taught those youngest to be real cautious about running away, as they came in blowing like a steam engine. Nope, no water yet as they were tied to a good stout post and curried down by the boss until he was ready for them to drink. Alex never let a team leave the farm that wanted to run away, and they remembered that for life. As Alex said, his mules were mated from birth, and he intended for them to stay that way.

We had a progression of farmers that wanted a good team. This brought on another point that Alex always looked into. Was the prospective buyer good to his team? A quick look at the buyer team always told the story. If his mules had any kind of whip marks on their hides, that buyer couldn't buy at any price. Hard? Yes, but that was the way my Alex did business. You be good to any animal and they will work for you.

The only time I ever felt sorry for a mule was a good neighbor of ours by the name of Swede. His mules were from the Mammoth strain. Work, you have never seen a better working pair, but the old dark side would come out in mid-afternoon. Hot, sultry, no wind, those mules would lay down in the traces and sulk! They wanted to stop for the day, roll in the dust, and have a good, long swig of water. This would put ole Swede back in Sweden speaking his unknown tongue. Picture this: In the middle of laying the corn by, lots of work to do, and your team is taking the rest of the afternoon off in the corn patch. Alex and I thought the scene funny as Swede spouted his tirade. His favorite saying was, "Vell, vell, ist teme to cook and let's eats me a mule."

How long the mules lay in the dirt was governed by how thirsty they were. Up they both would spring and run around and around the harrow, jawing to be heard for a mile. This trampled whatever crop into the ground, and Swede spit out this rest of his thoughts. It would take another hour getting that mess of mule flesh untied, and then it was past time to do the evening chores.

That red-faced Swede was fit to be tied when calm overcame him and his team.

"Halex, dem mules are maks me krazy. Day vant to lies in the dert ans sulks."

We had to look the other way and straighten our faces.

"Swede, there isn't anything wrong with your mules. They have you buffaloed and know it."

"Halex, you'd the ones dat's krazy. Deres nobodies dat could puts up wit dat."

"Tell you what, Swede. I bet I can break your mules of that habit in two sessions. If you do what I tell you, they will never lay down in the traces again."

"Halex, you yust names de prist."

"You go home and start working your mules this

afternoon, and I'll be over. We'll see what can be done."

Alex took his leather gloves and a couple of boys to help him with the erring mules and found Swede working around with a harrow.

"Howde, Halex, it won't bees long now. Days are yust bout to go down."

Alex didn't get to see the mules hit the dirt but heard ole Swede start in with his tirade. Alex got his gloves on and made two balls of cockleburs and went to look over those sorry mules in the dirt. Swede was a calling them all kinds of Swedish except a gentle cow.

Alex got the boys to hold up the tails of the mules and inserted a ball of burs you-know-where. After a few startled seconds, the mules exploded into a run around the harrow with their tails tucked in under them. That didn't help the mules any, as they wound the harness in a wad with legs sticking out all the way around. Alex and the boys got way back and let the show play on. Swede couldn't control the mules; the mules didn't want any help getting up, and it was time to quit for the day. The Loretts went home for the day and left ole Swede to get the burs out from under the mules' tails.

By the next morning ole Swede came over with the most docile team in the Cimarron Riverbend. Alex looked them over and mentioned, "I don't think they need another treatment of cockleburs, but just in case put a cocklebur plant on their collar, so those wild-eyed mules can see what is ready and try that for a while."

We heard from ole Swede later, and he was one happy farmer. He said the first time he hung a cocklebur plant on them they would look up over the shoulders with those brown eyes and start to tremble.

"Now, Swede, don't be mean to that good team of

Mammoth mules. They are real smart and will make you a good team."

"*Humph*," retorted ole Swede. "I's got a lazy wifes once a vhile, vill that work on her?"

Potato Home Brew

Along in the teens somewhere we had a bumper crop of potatoes. I canned all I could and still had plenty to feed the cows and horses. A real good neighbor from Germany was reputed to make good potato home brew, the kind that was fermented in a stone crock, bottled, let set in the root cellar, and ripen more. A lot of old-nesters were from Germany, and they could hold their liquor. The Swedes were something else. They drank until the supply was gone then went home walking a crooked line. Of course, my German Alex knew his limit and would get on his horse and find home in the middle of the night, or maybe his horse would find home. This started the different families making their own home brew, and everything went along pretty well until one of the Swedes bottled his potato brew too soon. He stored his bottles in the root cellar and went to bed. Those used beer bottles started to blow up in the middle of the night. Old Swede woke up and could only think of one thing. Somebody was stealing his home brew! We could only imagine what it sounded like, but that trip to the root cellar without shoes on was pure misery in his sticker patch. Swede inspected his loss and was leaving when more of the bottles exploded with a roar. This laid ole Swede out in the sticker patch face down with several shards of glass stuck you know where. Alex and two of his cronies brought wounded Swede to me the next morning. He had completely sobered up and was saying those words that come straight from over the waters.

"Oh, Hosie, come gets dis glass off me. Puts lots de salve on dese stickers. Doos anythings vickly!" If he had not been in such need, I would have laughed him off the farm, but this was too good to be true.

I washed up real good and got some of my strongest tincture of metholate I could find and dabbed his glass-filled rear end. I could have put on some soothing gel, but I didn't! We had the best two hours pulling glass and beer caps out of his backside, with him squealing like a fat pig.

The stickers in his feet and face have broken off, I thought. *He will have to let them work out.*

Of course, I didn't get all the glass out, and we got to do it all over again in a few days. I laughed at his pain, his cohorts laughed behind his back, and I got a promise that he would never make home brew again. I knew his drinking days were not over, but I let him believe that I was sorry for making him hurt. Ole Swede came over with a can of cream one day and thanked me for fixing him up. I didn't tell him I would have done it for nothing just so I could hear him squall! Alex needed some help, and here came Swede working like there was no tomorrow. Later, when they were hungry as hounds, I fed him up, and we talked about his home brew making.

"Hosie, you are the meanest voman valking disis erdt. You makest med hurts me on myd baks."

"Yes, Swede, I enjoyed that day working at your bare behind, and if you do that again, we'll have more fun."

He looked at me and I looked at that sorry hound and we both smiled our best. We proved that day that even in the worse of trials, neighboring was the best way to be.

Flour Mill

Every third day I would use ten pounds of flour, five pounds of coarse ground corn, and I don't have a clue how much rolled oats. A day was set aside once a month to go to the mill and restock those three staples. The day before Alex would give me one of the boys to fill the wagon box with shelled corn, three sacks of wheat, and two sacks of oats to be rolled. We would go to Yale and fill my grocery bill, have all that grain ground, and be back the same day. I would try to get a good head start to get in line at the mill. It didn't always work, but I could spend the time at the Yale Trading Post and get caught up with the news. My Louie was the driver of the day, and we looked forward to having some cheese and crackers for dinner. A good span of white mules would step right along until they got tired and then we had to keep prodding their hides to make time. We followed Mud Creek until we got to the cotton gin and the mill. The line was normal, people with the same idea as mine, but something was different. We could hear a loud droning noise, quiet, then that droning sound coming from a new building. Boy, the line was moving right along, and we were met with one of the mill operators.

"Hi, Grannie Josie, did you bring plenty of grain to grind today?"

I nodded above the din and asked what the noise all about was.

"Oh, Grannie, we got us a new hammer mill and grain roller. This will speed up your wait, and we can grind much more besides. Now, Grannie, you need to go into the office and pick out your sacks to put your house grain into. Louie and I will unload the wagon."

I stepped into a brand new office. I thought I was in a millinery shop and would you look at all the nice feed and flour sacks. I picked out a nice print, and the new manager, Mr. Allen, took my selection to the mill and promptly come back.

"Mrs. Lorett, do you want the same print each time you come back, or do you want to change?"

I right quick asked the question, "How much is all this going to cost?"

Mr. Allen spoke right up. "Oh, this is a service of the Yale Milling Company. There is no extra charge for these sacks. The only charge is if you want extra material to make shirts or curtains for your house."

I looked the material all over and brought a complete bolt of print. By the time I looked all this over, Louie came in and said he was loaded up and we could leave. I paid the bill and took my purchases to the wagon, examined all my new feed sacks, and could just see new shirts for all my boys.

My next stop at the Yale Trading Post we found

more sugar sacks made of unbleached material. Stocking up on sugar filled my bill; we bought cheese and crackers before dinner and we headed home. We were two miles from home before we ate our meal at Big Spring. We made home just in time for an afternoon nap. Alex came out to meet us and asked, "What is the matter?"

I tried to tell him about the new mill grinder, the new material I bought, and I was going to make into curtains, the sugar sacks, and ran out of breath. All that German would say was, "All right, okay, well, I am, do you suppose, of course, and why not?" He had agreed to the whole wagonload and never said a thing about it. I thought, *Well, I'll get right to my shirt making.* The boys all helped restock my flour, cornmeal, oat bins, and I started right in cutting out the first shirt for my youngest, John Clifford.

Alex announced the next morning that he had to go to Yale and pick up some hardware and asked if I needed anything. I kind of looked over my shoulder and said, "In all the hassle of the material, I forgot to get thread."

He spoke so softly, "Yes, Josie, I know. I was to supposed to have you pick up a big box of hardware and I forgot to put that on the list." We compared our list, made a new one, and Alex went on his way to Yale. I finished breakfast, spread the new material out on the dining room table, and went to work making eight new shirts for my men.

We were sitting down for dinner when Alex drove in. It was my turn to ask him why he was home so early.

"Josephine, you left this box at the Trading Post." I looked this wooden box over and told him, "Alex, that box was not at the post when I was there. What do you mean? Anyway, it's dinnertime. Come, let's eat and then we'll get back to work."

Alex picked at his beans and cornbread and confided he had eaten some crackers and cheese on the way home.

"Okay, Lorett, what have you got in the box?" He sent the boys after a hammer and nail bar and carefully took the box apart piece by piece. I could have taken that hammer to those slats and found out what we had, but no, not that old slowpoke. Whatever was in the box was covered with packing paper that he also saved. I caught a look at the very bottom piece and it looked like a treadle to me. I got down on my hands and knees and ripped the rest of the packing paper off and there stood a brand new Singer sewing machine. As I was gathering myself together, he produced all the thread I had sent for, a new pair of tailor scissors, and he set my new Singer beside the dining room table and said, "Sweet Josephine, sew to your heart's content. The boys and I will fix supper tonight."

I kept feeling the top and all the parts, the legs, and then I put the head up in place, threaded the belt and needle, and started its *click-a-dee clicking* that thrilled my heart. I grabbed all my menfolk and we had a group hug.

"Shoo, shoo all you kids, leave me alone. I will have a surprise later for you." I soon had shirts all the way around. I called the wild bunch in and we had a fitting, much to the delight of the smaller boys.

They fixed supper that night, and I ate my burnt offering sandwich. I never let on the bacon was stiff as hard tack; I would have eaten shoe leather and never said a word.

We never knew how the days would end. I set out to do a very stressful job (going to the mill) and got enough print material to make shirts all the way around. Alex brought me a new Singer, and I made eight men's shirts and me a new blouse.

I completed the shirts in time for the next Lord's Day. The only problem we had was, if the boys were standing way over there, I could not tell them apart. We called them "the bunch," and that tickled the whole family. I had to wash clothes the next week, and I very carefully washed all the new shirts together and hung them on the four-wire dryer, and I could just see them shrink! No problem, just pass the shirts down the line, and I made two more shirts, bigger this time, and we were the talk of the community. I used the sugar sacks for tablecloths, curtains, hand towels, you name it. When they were worn and thin, Alex used them for grease rags or I used them for washrags. My Singer sat beside me for five-and-a-half decades and sewed for all eighteen of my grands. As I remember, Alex paid $19.95 for my treasure. To be a homesteader, you had to be very resourceful and make a decision on the spur of the moment. I supposed the next thing would be bright lights so we could work all night long!

Indian Pine Tar

I was out of pine tar when Elf came over one day (she was not little anymore); her baby stuck out over her belt! She was out of pine tar too and asked if she could use our tar rock and a large iron kettle to cook off a batch. I had always let Old Man Sigh make my cough syrup, but the thought intrigued me.

"Elf, I don't have a tar rock, but you can borrow an iron pot any time."

"Oh, Grannie Josie, yes, you do have a tar rock, you just don't know where it is. Come out in your pasture, I'll show you."

We traipsed out where the sandstone rock come out of the ground. Elf took a brush broom and swept the top off, revealing a good-sized tar-spotted rock. The center was dish-shaped with a groove cut in the bottom that led to the side. I sat down on the edge, and Elf told me the story of tar rock.

"When we were forced to walk all the way from

Tennessee, we made camp on Pawnee Trail Spring that is on your land now, Grannie. Our men had lost all their arrows on the way and we had to make new ones. In fact, we chipped new arrowheads on this very rock. Grannie, if you will have the boys cut a fat pine tree, I will show you how to make pine tar."

This really got my interest up. I had never seen it, and here was a small Indian lady wanting to help me. I did not even know what a fat pine tree was. We made our way back to the house and fixed supper for the gang of hungered men. During the meal I just mentioned that I needed a fat pine tree cut and hauled down to the pine tar rock. All those fat-bellied boys could see was more work. Alex, always the father, knew that there was something in the wind and spoke like he knew what a fat pine tree was. All he said was, "Just show me what tree to cut and I will make that tree fall down in no time." The boys all groaned because they knew it involved them too.

We waited until the next morning, and Elf showed them what tree she had in mind. They cut it down and used the oxen to pull the tree to tar rock. We got an iron pot that held about ten gallons, and as soon as the fat pine tree arrived and was cut into chunks, Elf started right in filling the pot with stripes of heart wood. The next request was a bucket of red clay from the river; this we mixed with water until we had a good sticky mess to form a top to the grove in tar rock. By this time, the whole family was into the pine tar thing. All Elf had to do was make a request, and we filled in her wants. I had set a pot of beans the night before, and as soon as the top was finished for the channel, we ate dinner and the boys took a nap. We filled the iron pot with slivers of fat pine tree and turned the pot upside down over the channel. We took more clay and filled in around the bottom of the pot so no air could get into the fat pine stripes. I began to see what we were going to do, and by mid-afternoon the stage was set for making pine tar on our rock.

Elf said to let this sit until all the clay was hard, she would be back in a couple of days, and she would stay until we had our small crock full of pine tar. Alex and the boys kept looking at this strange goings-on and could only shake their heads. Elf came back, stacked cut wood completely around my iron pot, piled sticks on top, and started the cooking process; after a lot of hissing and smoke, pine tar oozed out into my stone crock ever so slowly. I took her food and water and she stayed the first night right beside her invention. I went out the next morning, and she said she was having contractions. I got my birthing kit and wasn't needed until in the night. I delivered a fine boy the size of her first girl, Tiny One. Elf nursed him that night while making pine tar. I tried to stay awake, but sleep put me in dreamland. I dreamed that I was going to have to spend the rest of my life sleeping on that rock. I awoke just at dawn and the fire had spent itself out. Elf had taken her share of the pine tar, her new son, and left for the tribe across the river. I was tired all over from the aches and pains of sleeping on a rock. My crock was half full of the best tar that nature could make; the only problem was, my iron pot could never be used to cook any food again. Oh well, in another fifty years I'll need more pine tar. Let's see now, that will make me 102 years old. Yep, I think I will need more by then.

BURNT OATMEAL CAKE

As I said before, you could hide a multitude of burnt offerings in oatmeal cake. All eight of my menfolk would eat me out of house and home if I were not careful. Little Elf and her brave husband came one day to make cake in a Dutch oven. We finished with the mixing and had the cake out over a small campfire in the yard. I do not remember what kind of soup we had that day, but those boys ate all my sourdough bread and sopped the soup pan out. By this time, Little Elf and I were working on a quilt top and the menfolk were on their own after dinner. We had forgotten about the cake in the Dutch oven, not my men. They discovered the cooking pan that smelled like cake and helped themselves to its contents. They washed the whole meal down with fresh milk that had been cooling down in the cistern and left us with the dishes. I remembered the yard-cooked cake and made a mad dash to save what I could and only found a slicked out pan. Let me tell you, it was not me who got mad. That little ole Indian squaw got to kicking sticks out in the yard, saying those Cherokee words, and ran her husband all the way to the barn. All I could do was sit down on the back stoop and laugh. Little Elf came back from chasing her man, flopped down beside me, and said the words of the day.

"I've wanted to get mad at him for a week. Suppose that will have to do. Oh, Grannie Josie, that husband of mine is more like your white men every day!"

We burst out laughing, not in front of the men.

Hillbillies

Right after the run of '93, we had a family of hillbillies move into a homestead close to the river. They said they were from Arkansas and to hear them talk about cracked us up. I think they were all good people except a couple of the boys they hid out all the time. I do not mean to say they were in trouble with the law or anything like that, but the boys did not look right. I was over across the river to a family of girls that had the itch and came back by the Strangs family. Of all the shouting you have ever heard when my Blackie pulled me in under their shade trees, I could not make heads or tails of what was being said. There were boys running out the back door, women screaming at the kids, dogs barking, an ole donkey was making his voice heard, and Old Man Strangs come slipping around the house. I was ready to make dust when the old man spoke up in his drawl.

"Why, howdy thar, Mizz Josie., I see you's been out for a drive wid yo black hoss."

I very cautiously said, "Yes, Mr. Strangs, I—"

"Plez, Mizz Josie, calls me Ben, and you gets down and sits a spell. Susie you'll comes out heah. We's got company from ova ta holler!

So help me I had to hold my ears, he was so loud, and the sweetest little grannie woman comes out of the house with a jar full of cool spring water.

"Oh, Ben, don't be so loud. You'll scare Mizz Josie offa her perch."

I knew right then I was at the right place, Loud Mouth Ben and all.

Susie and I sat on the front of the porch; there was not a chair to be found. I sipped the jug very cautiously and found it was sugar water. Oh, what a delight, sitting in the shade a talking with my neighbors, drinking sweet water. The family got over their fright and filed back in pell-mell and sat with us. We visited about the weather, and I kept hearing music in the house so I asked Susie about it.

Susie very quietly said her boys were tuning up for a sing and for all our family to come and join in.

"Susie, have the boys come out now. I would like to hear them."

Susie looked over the way and asked if I would be scared of her boys.

"Susie, I'm a midwife, and I have seen everything. There is nothing here to be scared of."

"Mizz Josie, are you sure? My boys don't look real good!"

I assured Susie again to have them sit with us; I wanted to hear their music.

The shock I received that day made my heart bleed.

All the boys had a red rash that spread in their hair, both ears, and eyes. The boys were blind as night. They filed out so slow, bumping into each other, and sat with us on the porch, ground, and some stood. I could count six, and they said there were two more who stayed inside. I did not venture to ask about their looks.

I heard the sweetest music that afternoon. There was not an instrument of any kind except a Jew's harp and mouth organ. They sang and played all the old hymns that are forever, a good rendition of "Chicken in the Bread Pan Picking Out Dough," "Fire on the Mountain," and several I didn't know. I finished my jug of sweet water and said, "Susie, have the boys been looked at by a doctor?"

"Oh no, Mizz Josie. We don't have the money."

"Susie and Ben, I don't charge anything. Would you like for me to look at your family?"

Ben spoke up rather quickly and told me not to bother, for I might catch whatever they had.

"Ben, you or Susie don't seem to have anything wrong with you. I don't think it's contagious."

"But Mizz Josie, we don't have any money. Besides that, we don't know what con-tag-a-ous is!"

I spoke very quietly and gave those the best hillbilly talk I could think of.

"Youinss ain't kotched nuttin'. I just want to hep yo kids!"

You should have seen that couple brighten up when they found out I understood their plight.

I asked for water to wash my hands, and Susie took me around to the horse trough, gave me some lye soap, and said, "Hep yosef." I washed up outside the tank and asked to see one of the youngest boys there beside the horse trough.

"Why, Mizz Josie, come into my house."

"No, Susie, you don't understand. I want to see these kids out in the sunlight."

"Wall, okay, but the sunlight hurts their eyes and they cry out so at night."

"Yes, you are right, Susie, but I need them outside here where you and me can see them real good."

She finally relented and told Ben to send the youngest to me. I knew this was going to be hard, but I wasn't prepared for the sight. The boy was whimpering when he come around the corner and buried his face in his mother's lap. I pulled his hair back and it came out in my hand; his scalp was a mess of swollen flesh about as red as canned beets.

"Susie, I need for you to hold this boy so I can look into eyes." They weren't any better, so red it even made my hands start to sting.

"Susie, let this young'n go back to the porch, and I'll come back around there and I want to see some of the older boys." My hands were a mass of stinging by this time, so I washed up again and they stung more. I looked at two more kids and saw the same thing. I tried to wash up again but my hands were hurting so bad. I went back around to the horse trough and smelled of the water. "Hmm, Ben and Susie, come around to the back of the house. I don't see any horses or mules around this water, why not?"

Ben spoke up with, "Mizz Josie, we don't have any stock. That water is our wash water and we clean up here."

"Ben, when do you change that water?"

"We, ah, ah, use the water until it rains, and then we empty it out and refill it with water from off the house."

"Okay, Ben and Susie, let's go out along the river and get me some yucca plant. My hands are about to burn off!"

Blackie took us down on the sandbar. I soon found my soap plant, washed in the river water, and almost at once the sting was gone.

"Okay, Ben and Susie, this is going to be hard to believe, but that water in your tank is bad. You are washing with lye soap and rinsing off the soap in the water. The lye gets so stout it about takes the hide off your kids. Now why it don't hurt you I don't know, but we got to get all the clothes off them boys, take them down to the river, and give them a bath with that yucca soap plant. Let me take you back to your house and you do their baths. I got to go home and get me some soothing gel and I'll be back in the morning before daylight. I have to get a look at the rest of those eyes right smart."

I do not know if I did any good talking to Ben and Susie, but we had a good understanding. I got in after dark and left the next morning way before daylight. Old Blackie seemed to know just where to go. All the family was sitting on the front porch in the same clothes as yesterday. I took a coal oil lantern, started from the oldest to the youngest, and held their eyes open and filled them full of the cactus gel that I had made up. I made up a pan full of black straw tea and made the whole family drink at least a cup full except Ben and Susie. Wasn't long before the kids started drifting off to bed. Ben and Susie couldn't believe what was going on; their family was actually going to bed.

As the sun started up, we all took a nap on the front porch and I got acquainted with hard-time living, with and without. We left the family asleep, and Ben, Susie, and I took a walk about on the riverbanks. They asked me what I had put in the kids' eyes. I very quietly took them to a special cactus plant, broke off a spear, and told them to put the gel in their eyes. They were amazed that green plants could hold healing powers. I told them about the wonders of the earth that the Lord had made, how in speaking to the earth all the plants grew. In speaking to the air, all the birds were made. I just told them about the Lord, how they needed to serve him. Ben and Susie knelt down right there in the sand and asked the Lord to forgive them of their sins and to come into their hearts. They arose and we walked back to their home on the banks of the Cimarron River. As we were walking back to their house, they confessed why the soap never bothered them.

"We's nava washed in the tank. After dark eva night we's sipped down to the river and washed in da cool waters."

I went back to their home a couple of more times and found the family better each time; it was so refreshing to see them start to see again, playing their mountain music to all who wanted to hear. We got in a bind at harvest, and there came ten more mouths to feed. They helped until they caught us up, and we had a musical each day at noon. Susie cooked one of her special possum soup dinners; I made four pans of cornbread just in case somebody found out what she had cooked. Believe me, there was not one sopping left. Payment for midwife? It was never brought up. We were a neighbor that needed help, and they happened to be close by. Best kind of payment.

Yale Picnic

We worked on that ole sandhill farm from dawn till can't, accepting the day whether dry, wet, cold, or hot, always doing something to improve. The news came that Yale was going to have a picnic for everybody who had made the land run into Indian Territory. As it turned out, we planned to spend at least two or three days camped under the wagon, cook all our food over an open fire, see the sights, and try to keep track of the boys. Alex and boys found all my cooking irons in the barn; rust had taken them over, the iron pots and skillets had potted flowers in them, and besides that, it was hot! It took us a week to get everything ready, but by Thursday morning we set out for Yale with a team of white mules pulling the wagon and the boys riding their horses. We arrived south of Main Street and tried to get into the shade. All the good spots had already been taken up with drink stands and campers just like us. We set upwind from all that smoke we expected. It was a good thing; there must have been one hundred wagons that came in that night. We ate breakfast Friday morning, and a paper was circulated around that told about what was going to happen through Sunday. The boys complained about rusty-looking things in their eggs that morning, and I told them it was probable fly specks; they were so hungry they would have eaten the shells too.

We separated and were going to meet for dinner back at the wagon; we all got busy and most of us didn't make it till suppertime. I had fixed a big pot of ham and beans before we left the farm; I bought crackers and filled them up on what was warmed up. I don't know who started telling about the fat man in the circus, but I got all over them for making fun of someone. Alex intervened with, "Oh, Josie, let them boys alone. I saw the signs and it said that guy weighted 365 pounds. That can't be right. Look around at all these farmers. There can't be anybody that weights much over 150. Their scales are wrong. Anyway, they are going to have the guy walk down to the cotton gin and we'll know tomorrow how much he weighs."

The other talk was a sword-swallowing act, a woman who could hang by the hair of her head, some mangy-looking monkeys, a few little horses, and two peacocks. I wondered then if we would ever get those boys back to work hoeing cotton. I sat another pot of beans for Saturday and made the mental note to look up some of my neighbors. We woke up right at the crack of dawn and felt like a wagon had run over us while sleeping on the ground. We ate the last of the sourdough bread that morning with jelly, I gave each one of the boys a dime to get a hot dog for dinner, and we said we would meet at dark for supper at our wagon.

Visiting the wagons was hard and slow. I met all our neighbors, and of course we had to talk at the same time. Susie Strangs and I walked together; the town was completely filled with wagons, people, and horses. We couldn't walk along the stores for the people along them. We had to walk out in the street and risk getting trod on by somebody's mules. If we missed anybody we couldn't tell. After our hot dog for dinner, the most awful commotion began out in the street. I thought it must have been a moving fight from the dust being kicked up. Turned out to be the fat man walking to the cotton gin. As he walked by me, I thought, *Boy, that guy has gained weight overnight.* Susie and I couldn't help ourselves; we got right in behind the throng.

The mayor was there and gave a political speech, and the constable was there with a lost child that the mother claimed in mid-sentence. The City of Yale was going to cook and serve pancakes wrapped in paper at the park where we were camped for Sunday breakfast. Here we were standing in the hot sun, and finally the fat man stepped up to the scales and the mayor stopped him and said, "The scales aren't big enough!"

You should have heard the groan.

"No, I was just kidding. Tiny stepped on the scales." You could have heard a pin drop when the weight master said, "Three hundred seventy-four pounds, a new record!" The cheering didn't stop for two minutes; we had never seen such a person.

I got back to my cooking and cooked off our mess of beans and made cornpone bread. I was glad we had filled our water bucket at the pump in front of the bank because we drank that too. The boys scattered like flies and didn't come in till dark. We were so tired, we plopped down under our wagon like a bunch of hogs and slept the night through. I woke early, stiff as a board, and could hear the breakfast pancakes brigade banging on dish pans: "Come and get it!"

We struggled ourselves out from under the wagon and tried to look make ready for those pancakes. We looked a mess! The only good thing was, I didn't have to feed several hundred hungry farmers. They had set a big piece of steel plate up on rocks and lit a fire that would have burnt down a building. The fire soon died down, and the line formed a block long and the paper-wrapped pancakes went out by the handfuls. They fed as long as anybody was in line and some besides. My boys must have eaten six or eight apiece. I ate so much I was ashamed of Alex, and the singing started for church service. All the Strangs family was standing up in a wagon, and the people gathered around to the best singing I had ever heard.

This must have gone on for an hour, and W.H. Fritch climbed up in the wagon and told all the people to sit the best they could and he would bring the Word of God that Sunday morning. I can't say how long he preached, but you could have heard a pin drop at any one time. We wound up standing up and shouting praises to God. He settled everyone down and prayed for the people, the churches in Yale, the town of Yale, and the President of the United States. A color guard from WW1 unfurled the United States flags, and the Strangs family led everybody in the "Star-Spangled Banner." A cheer went up that you could hear all over town, and plans were made to have the Yale Picnic ever year from then on.

We slam-banged our picnic gear into our wagon and started for home. The boys outran us and were gathered around the dining room table as soon as we got in.

"What do you boys want?"

In chorus they exclaimed, "We want some real food."

I held them as long as I dared and made a deal.

"If you boys will take the wagon and all my pots and pans down to the river and sand scour them till bright, then take a bath yourselves and put on clean clothes, I will cook fried chicken, biscuits, gravy, and all the spring water you can drink. Oh, and by the way, wash the wagon out too. It stinks like dirty people."

They groaned and got on the way as Alex and I took a quick bath on the porch in cold water, changed clothes, and the farm got back to normal in about a week. I thought we were over the Yale Picnic until one day I saw four boys hanging on the cotton scales set at four hundred pounds. Oh well!

Well

I had bucketed water all my life. First was springs along the way, drank out of cow tracks, sopped brackish water with a rag to cool my brow, took a bath in a seep in the side of a hill, stood out the rain ... I can't think of them all but anything to get the grime off my hide. The very best was a cistern that was beside the back door: Walk right outside, crank up a bucketful, and throw it on your husband. Let me tell you, that water was cold and wet when it came the other way.

Now the problem, if you lived in Oklahoma, you would run out of cistern water in the summertime with no rain! No problem on my part. I'd just catch a big, strappin' boy, give him two buckets, point him to the nearest spring, and listen to him complain! I put up with that tirade just so long and would get another boy. Let's see now, seven days in a week, seven boys, well that comes out about right.

"Oh, Momma, let so-and-so go this time."

"Nope, it's your day, so get to hoofing it to the spring, boy!"

I let this get on my nerves and had Alex go get water one day, and he only brought back one bucket.

"Here, boy, I need two buckets of water!"

He right quick smarted off and the battle was on. We didn't talk to each other the whole blessed day. The boys got real quiet and walked around us not saying a word.

I think back now, but I should have gone and got the water myself, but I wasn't going to give an inch. I went to my Singer sewing machine and promptly broke my last needle; Alex went to the blacksmith shop, started a fire in the forge, and burnt his hand. Dinnertime came and went, and I was not going to fix a bite to eat. The smaller boys started whining about starving to death; the older ones went to the neighbors and begged a sandwich. This was not a good day for the Loretts. I heard a commotion in the kitchen and found six buckets of water setting around all carried by Alex himself. I relented and fixed my bunch supper and all seemed to be well, except one thing. I felt I was entitled an apology. My nonspeaking family was still a mess of confusion, and we didn't have an evening prayer. That was the final straw!

The row started between the boys, and boiled out in the open between Alex and I. We got to slinging pillows at each other, the boys, my cat, the dogs, and we got to clean house. We settled down and let the boys come set on the back porch very quietly. By this time Alex and I were smiling at each other to see the downtrodden look on those poor little things we called boys. We left that bunch out on the back porch and got two buckets of water and threw it all over them. You should have seen their surprised looks. They in turn got us wet and we called that our bath for the night.

End of story. *No!* I really thought everything turned out okay with the rain that filled the cistern the next day. We had water by the bucketful right by the back door. A man came the next day looking for a team of mules; they walked out to the barn, around the house, checked the cistern, and shook hands.

I thought, *We have sold another span of mules.* Wasn't but a day or two until a big machine came and set up just east of our house and downhill a ways. Of all the ripping and roaring coming from one truck, I couldn't think what was going on until the first stick of pipe went into the hole. Alex had made a deal for a well to be drilled on our land between the house and the barn!

I don't know who was thrilled the most, the boys, Alex, or me. I couldn't take my eyes off that drill pipe. I left all the work to you-know-who and went about my housekeeping. That ole truck drilled its way plumb down to the level of the Cimarron River and struck an ocean of pure, clean water. They set pipe the next day with a pump on the bottom, set up a derrick that stuck way up in the air, then put up the biggest wind-mill on top. I'll never forget the wind-pumped water spilling out on the ground. We all gathered around, and you guessed it, we threw water on the whole tribe. While the well men were at our house, they ran a line to the cistern, barn, and blacksmith shop, and to an overhead tank so we could take a shower. I think Alex called the overhead tank sun-heated. I still had to carry water from the cistern to the back porch, all of ten feet; I guessed I could make that sacrifice. Of course, our water dog boys played in the horse tank, but what the heck, we had water on the farm!

Sooners

Before the run of '93, the United States of America called us Sooners. The militia ran through every hollow in Payne County chasing, actively engaging those bands of nesters. I know we should have been thrown out on our tin ear for being there too soon, but I was part Indian and they left us alone. I know that didn't make it right, but we used any scheme to exist. We had sold a perfectly good tree farm in Missouri to build our dream house on the hill. The Government of the United States had all but stolen our existence to be an Indian in the eastern states. We slogged ourselves to Oklahoma and set up housekeeping on that ole sandhill farm to get away from persecution. We settled in and stayed the course, not liking the outcome, but here we were. I knew the old Indian ways of existing off the land and loved every moment. That lifestyle was not to be had in Oklahoma; there were way too many people to live off the land, and the land had to be worked to exist. I'm proud that we were able to make the run of '93. We had the resources that made that happen and will have to live with the knowledge that we were Sooners and be proud of it. Most of the nesters had some kind of angle that they used to claim the land. Some even had scars of fights dating to '93, tales of Indian raids that turned out to be toughs of another race. People did what they needed to do to hold on and make one more crop. Lives were shortened, sacrificed, and dedicated to proving up the land. I'm not making excuses, complaining, or bragging; making the run was the hardest task we ever did in our lives, but we held onto the land to settle our end of Payne County, Oklahoma, September 16, 1893.

BEDBUGS

I think I should tell you the worst case I had ever seen of those bloodsuckers. This couple slept together as normal couples do. I have no problem with that; it's the Lords way, and I'm not going any farther. This lady was so poor, her dress just hung on her bones, and I thought that if she sneezed,she would have been undressed. I didn't get too concerned until she complained that she always had blood spots all over the sheets in the morning.

"People, wake up! That can only be bedbugs!" I very quietly said, "I will come over to your house and we will see where the suckers are hiding."

"No, no, Granny Josie, we're all right. My José don't have a spot on him."

I mulled that over and thought, *I don't think so.*

"Now, Emma Lou, you don't look to be right pert. There's something trying to eat the hide off your body."

Finally she agreed to let me look at their bed and maybe something could be done.

I took my Blackie and wore old clothes. José met me out on the porch, and I could see right away a fine specimen of Italian decent. You know, short, squatty potty, smoked big cigars all the time, ate plenty of garlic, and smelled the same. True to Emma Lou's word, José was in good shape, not a blood spot on what I could see of his shiny hide. I went into the bedroom and found little ole Emma Lou bloodstarved, close to death! She started in with, "Oh, Grannie Josie, there's nothing wrong with me. I'm just tired plumb out."

"Emma Lou, get yourself up off that bed. Those bedbugs are going to kill you," just as she passed out.

I called José and told him to carry his wife outside and try to get some breakfast down her.

As the couple was preoccupied with breakfast, I lifted one corner of the mattress cover, and the straw-filled rag was moving! I dropped the cover and backpedaled outside and felt like there were a million that had jumped on me. As reason prevailed, I remembered that in the daytime all bedbugs go back to their homes in the straw. I went back to the mattress and lifted the side where José slept; not one bug. I started to scratch my scalp to help me think and remembered the colony of bedbugs that were in the bed.

By that time I heard Emma Lou talking and I asked her, "How long has the straw-filled mattress been used?"

"Oh, Grannie Josie, I can't remember. Must be eight or ten years, why?"

"José, do you sleep with your wife?"

"Why sure, Grannie. Why shouldn't I?"

I introduced ole Italian born to his family of bedbugs and said, "We need to burn the critters."

José eyes about popped out of his head and he asked
the question, "Grannie Josie, why don't those buggers
get on me?"

"José, I don't know yet, but let's start a fire out in
the yard and we'll carry this mob to a fiery death."

"Grannie Josie, this is not your problem. Let me
carry that mattress outside."

I right quick said, "Yes, José, that's a good idea!"

José and I doused the floor, bed, and side walls with
coal oil to kill the bedbugs. I went home the short-
est way possible and caught my menfolk all out in the
fields.

You've got it, I undressed right there in front of
God and washed, scrubbed, rubbed, my hide with lye
soap until it shone like a mirror, dressed in a towel,
and went inside. There sat my Alex with the worst-best
smile on his face.

"Josie, you will not believe what I have just seen out
in my backyard—"

"Oh, shut up, you, you . . ." I couldn't think of what
was the worst, those bedbugs or that silly grin on his
face. I got my everyday clothes on and a good apron and
felt some better. I fixed some dish that had garlic in it,
and then it hit me why José didn't have a bite on him.
Between the cigar and garlic, the bedbugs didn't like
him! All this was bad, but I had to go over the next day
and tell José about the cure for bedbugs. Now imagine
this; I fried up a good mess of liver and left ole José
hand-feeding Emma Lou fresh fried liver and onions
with plenty of garlic. I gagged all the way home.

Roarin' Twenties

Eastern Payne County was the center of the oil boom in Oklahoma. We had been living on our farm for twenty-seven years, scratching out a living from the land. As Alex often said, we were work brittle to the core. Our family was married out except Lambert and John Clifford by the twenties. They all lived close by, and we had a yard full of grands running those sandhills. We loved the challenge and lived for the Sundays when most of them came around. We never knew how many would be home, so I always cooked plenty with a double batch of bread and watched it disappear. The oil boom brought changes to our lifestyle that you wouldn't believe.

Let's take Yale. Oil fields were being discovered daily, and I don't mean little stripper wells, but gushers of oil that came out of the ground free for hauling it away. This was just one of many fields coming on line. Cushing, Oilton, Drumright, Silverton, Yale, Marmac, Quay, Jennings, Stillwater, with refineries at Drum-

PAT LORETT

right, Cushing, and Yale. I wouldn't attempt to count
the team and wagon freight lines that hauled nothing
but oil. Pipe line and pump stations were being built as
fast as they could be fabricated. We lived on our side
of the Cimarron River and let the world do its thing. I
should have known there was change in the air.

Louie, our good ole Louie, bought the first trucks
to be had, and started his own trucking business hauling oil field equipment. One truck, one driver, no
exceptions; this was the beginning of the Lorett Brothers Trucking Company. All told there were five of my
boys herding those trucks anywhere there was a location. Sometimes they were gone a week at a time, then
a month, then Alex and I were alone for long periods.

The oil companies leased our quarter section of
land; the first oil well was drilled up in our woods pasture where there was plenty of wood to feed the boiler.
It must have taken six or seven months to drill, but I
remember the day they brought our first gusher on line.
We didn't get any work done by watching the oil flow
downhill and completely cover our spring with black,
sticky crude. We gawked in disbelief as our precious
water supply was destroyed in one afternoon. People
and animals drank that water, we swam to our heart's
content for centuries on end, and all we could see were
a few cattails sticking up through the muck. I went
into the house seething mad at the mess that oil had
brought to our farm. I vowed right then never to have
anything to do with that devil called black gold.

Alex came in saying that the oil company said they
would clean up everything as soon as all the drilling
was done. He could see my anguish and tried to soothe
the beast in me. I asked if we could run the bunch back
across the Cimarron River, and he produced the lease

agreement that stated they could drill as much as they wanted. Signed by both of us, dated, and witnessed! Oil immediately started moving by mules and tank wagons to the refineries. The drillers punched more wells, and they all made their mess in turn. How many tanks of oil they hauled from our oil strike I never knew. They could have taken it all back if we could have had our clean farm back. Our water well east of our house continued to produce good clean water, which was a blessing, and we survived as always, just existing.

We were almost out of the farming business as far as row crops and hay. Alex sold most of our mules, turned our oxen out in the big pasture, butchered all the beef stock, and sold them out of the back of our wagons to the oil patch workers. The apple orchard was a blessing; we didn't make a good crop every year, but when we did there was a ready demand for whatever we wanted to sell. Alex and I didn't need much, but with the boys gone we had to let the farm go back to weeds. We tried to worry ourselves into keeping the fields mowed but had to give that up also. We banked all the oil and farm money; all the expenses we had were taxes and what food we had to buy. We saw the oil boom come and go on our farm. It was none too soon for me, but Alex tried to make do with what he understood, existing.

The oil stopped coming out of the ground ... surprise! I could have danced a jig for a week on end when the flow stopped never to start again. Something about there were so many wells being pumped that the whole field collapsed was the word from the oil companies, and *poof!* they were gone. They ran off and left all the tanks, equipment, lines, and the spilled oil. Our spring was the worst disaster on the farm, and I finally turned the whole mess over to the Lord. I sure couldn't fix that kind of a wreck. Our oil checks stopped, the tank wagons were silent, and quiet regained its hold on our farm. Seemed so strange all that steam equipment was silent, and the smell was going away. We had a huge rain one night and the spring looked some better. Alex and I got the lease contract out and reread the clause where all the spilled oil would be cleaned up. As it turned out, that contract wasn't worth the paper it was written on. I tried to get mad again and the only thing I got was a headache. We had several big rains that spring, and I saw a surprise in the spring. Cattails were coming back. All traces of oil sludge had been washed down the Cimarron. I got down on my knees that day and remembered what I had turned over to the Lord. Oh, me of little faith as I cried my eyes red.

I was never so glad for anything to be over in our bend of the Cimarron River. Other towns raged on for decades with the problems brought on by oil. There was one thing that I liked about the oil boom. Alex bought a Model-T Ford car and taught himself to drive. We could drive into Yale, have one of those new things called a hamburger, and be home before dark. It cost me twenty cents for gasoline, fifty cents for two hamburgers ... *humph,* we wouldn't get to go too much at that price. The oil boom was an exciting time in our lives, but I wouldn't want to go through it again. When poor times come along, don't fret. Give the Lord the praise and some good will come out of those trials.

Lambert and Alpha brought their daughter, Ruth, to me to keep for a few days. They were in the midst of moving to another location and were busy beyond belief. I think they said that in Seminole, Oklahoma, a big oil discovery was being developed. Of course, my granddaughter Ruth and I got along famously and played the days till dark. I began having chest pains, and Alex had to feed and take care of Ruth. Then Alex started the same thing. We were sure glad when Alpha came and got their child. After a few days we were some better, and I figured out that lifting those grands will make your arms, back, heart, and head ache, but it sure was worth it.

Alex tried to farm, but the years had taken its toll on his body. He kept working with his mules and sold enough to pay the taxes on our land.

OCTOBER 1929

We didn't get the news for a week that the stock market
had crashed. To show how dumb we were, we didn't
even know who that was! I wrote the date down and
asked around when the funeral was. Nobody knew in
the riverbend area. A month later we found out the
economy of the United States had collapsed and that
hard times were sure to come. I thought, *Well, what's
new about that news?*

We had lived so hard with our noses to the grind
stone that the stone was about worn out. Anyway, the
boys straightened us out with the statement that we
were not to spend money on anything. As the saying
goes, we sewed our purse strings tight and buckled
down to the task at hand. The farm would produce
anything we wanted to plant, but there in lay the problem. No help, no boys to plow, plant, hoe, or harvest.
Alex and I gathered all the labors around the empty
harvest table, and we looked at each other. The taxes

were due in a few months, we had to eat, and that was the sum of our labors.

We started in the next spring with as much garden as we could work, which was not much! Of course, we tried to do everything like old times and got ourselves so sore we couldn't touch our muscles with a powder puff. I thought I would get back to making our own bread and made the biggest mess. I was glad for our ole hound dogs; they ate like kings that day. I tried again, and Alex complained that the taste was good but it was sure tough. *Humph!* Let that buzzard get hungry and I bet he will learn to soak his bread in some soup. Yes! That is the answer when you are getting old, stoop-shouldered, cranky, and smooth-mouthed—soak your food!

We slipped back into hard times like we had never been gone. The mule crop was good, and we got used to working again. I remembered the oil days, and that was all I wanted to remember. We ate the first radishes of the season like old times and filled in our days working just enough to get by. We had to pay our taxes in two installments, but let me tell you, we paid them. We heard of many old-nesters who had to move on and leave everything but the clothes on their backs. We had visions of moving on, but to where? There was nothing left anywhere to house us or to make a living. Our boys were all so good to help, but they were having families too. They did the next best thing: they brought those grands to us to try to scratch us out a living. I think Alex and I got the best end of the bargain. All we had to do was make bread by the tub full and spoil those grands.

My Alex had been failing for a period of time, and old age caught him June 7, 1931, a very black day in my life. All my boys gathered around me in Greenwood Cemetery, and we said the final good-byes to a good husband, father of seven boys, grandfather to lots of grandchildren, and friend to all the old-nesters in the Cimarron Riverbend. We gave my husband of forty-four years a Christian burial, and I started a new era in my life.

ALONE

After Alex was gone, I asked myself, *What will I do? Where will I go?*

The fact that I couldn't live on my own farm was finally answered by my boys. Lawrence, Virginia, and their four boys would take over the old homestead, and I could stay with them. I made one change that seemed to satisfy everybody: Let me pack a suitcase, and I would do some traveling to my boys' homes wherever they lived. I was so upset. I don't know who I visited first, but I always had that itchy feeling to move on. I visited all the way around and couldn't seem to stick in any one place. I guessed I was just too independent for my own good.

Lambert and Alpha came to me and said, "Mother, let's get you a small place in Yale, close to the Methodist church. Maybe you can make friends and settle down."

To the relief of everyone, I did just that and spent

many a sleepless night moaning over my plight. I did go to church and joined their fellowship. At least that give me somebody to talk to. I started back to my tatting and quilt making. My hands were so stiff at first, but I soon found myself crooning those nameless tunes of long ago and making do.

You know, Josie, I said to myself, *if you would join the church, maybe the Lord could help you get over the doldrums.*

I tried, oh, I tried to find my string of beads, to no avail. I just couldn't think where I put them. It took a good sleep and a deep dream to remember. I had gotten mad at Alex and threw them at him, never to be seen again. I was so ashamed at transgressing against the Lord for being mad. Finally, I prayed for forgiveness and forgot all about the beads. This church didn't use prayer beads; the pastor was not a priest. They believed in the Lord, so I turned over a new leaf in my life and settled down in the Methodist church of Yale, Oklahoma.

Each time I had company after that, I wanted to get out of sight. Selfish? Well, maybe, but I was known to be a cranky thing and life got straightened out for me.

President Roosevelt signed the first Social Security bill in 1935. It was several years later that I received my first check for twenty-four dollars. That really surprised me, but the best part was, I got that check each month for the rest of my life. My boys had been paying my rent, and now I was able to pay that eight dollars dollars a month myself. It was along there sometime that my grandson Pat started coming to Yale to the Harding School. He was my youngest grandson and a blond-headed ball of sweat. I always could depend on a wet hug from that kid, and we got along famously. He always came by to see me whenever they brought him to town. One thing that kind of bothered me was his questions. He could ask the oddest thing, and I caught him writing my answers down in his Big Chief writing tablet. He always had a black streak on his tongue from licking the end of his indelible pencil.

There were parts of my life that I wasn't proud about, and that scamp found my name in the family Bible. I told him what I wanted him to know and erased the Indian part away. I encouraged his efforts and thought the matter settled. Little did I know that years later he would write a family history about the Loretts and tell about me. Oh well, somebody might get to know about the Lord and what he has done for my life.

SHORTY

I met Pat's sweetheart sometime the first part of 1952. She looked so young at fifteen, but I could tell they were meant for each other. Saturday nights they would come by and visit with me on their date. I can't remember her name; everybody just called her Shorty. I thought, *How quaint,* but her personality came through and she was a hugger just like Pat. The very best thing that I liked about the child was she knew how to quilt and would make a few handstitches with me on my ever-present quilt rack.

Before the light goes out of my life, I want to hand my life's feather quill to Pat so he can write my epitaph. Pat, write about the hard, good, turbulent, disappointing, lean times in my life. Tell about me not serving the Lord, repenting, and getting back into the good graces of Jesus Christ. Tell about the people I have witnessed to, and how many I missed telling about the Lord. Pat, use my life to glorify the Lord any way you can.

I am in the Yale Hospital now, and I don't remember who my boys are. They all met with me this morning, and I told them that if I can't eat through my own mouth to let me go to ever be with my Lord. I felt the last beat of my heart this afternoon and realized then I didn't need it any more.

END OF AN AGE

My Grandmother Josephine Wilhelmina Owen-Smith Lorett passed on to ever be with the Lord in 1954. I take up her life's feather quill and tell the life of an old-nester who had the gumption to strike out with her husband and make the Indian Territory Land Run in Oklahoma, September 16, 1893. I have replaced that feather quill with a computer and told to best of my knowledge that lifetime of happenings. Yes, I filled in the spaces where there were no written words or pictures. Dates, places, and names are as close to the census records I can find. Please forgive me when I made mistakes. I have asked the Lord to help me use her witness to glorify his own name. I give all the credit to my ancestors who made the sacrifices to settle the land and prove it up. I thank you for reading along with me as I present *To 1944, 1945 and Beyond*, and *To My Own Home*. This is the end of the age of my ancestors and their lives that made it possible for me to be here today.

PAT A. LORETT